I0726971

Love Simply

A book of

Poems

Short Stories

& *Nonsense*

(with a little help from the kids)

And Featuring

The Nascar Nag

Douglas A. Alberts

Manzanita Writers Press

ISBN: 978-1-952314-92-6
LCCN: 2023907905

Manzanita Writers Press
manzapress.com
manzanitawp@gmail.com

Cover photography:
Douglas A. Alberts and Patricia Kalfsbeek
Author photo: Patricia Kalfsbeek
Layout graphic design and cover design:
Aaron Cameron
CameronBookForge.com
Cameroncreative.co

This collage of writings is the result of sixty-plus years of
life experiences. Over time those tidbits of knowledge,
those ideas, those discoveries, and those experiences began
to accumulate at an astonishing rate, especially in the latter
years.

In order to create a legacy, the author began to put them
together, to write something that could be shared and
enjoyed.

On these pages you may discover intimate portraits of
life. Surprises are ahead as each page is turned. Expect the
unexpected ("Do trees really sneeze?")

Herein is prose and poetry, as well as stories of love and
adventure, many based on true life happenings. These
carefully worded items will touch your emotions. So if you
cry or laugh out loud, enjoy the experience. The journey
awaits.

Tsunami

I was sitting there, hardly paying attention to the tiny waves at my feet, watching them come and go . . . but unknown to me, a gigantic earthquake rumbled into existence way out to sea. The water rose to a mighty crescendo, headed toward where I sat. By the time it reached me, it was a tsunami, greater than any in history. It turned my life upside down, engulfed me in feelings and experiences I'd never before known. I still tumble about in the midst of that upheaval, not wanting to escape, even looking to drown in the depths of these experiences.

You, my darling, are that tsunami.

Special thanks to Blondie

For her encouragement

For her support

But most of all . . .

For her love.

Table of Contents

IN MEMORY OF
MY SON
DOUGLAS MARK ALBERTS
1958-1967
AND
MY WIFE
IRIS SUE ALBERTS
1939-2017

Words

I am *ENCHANTED* by your very presence.

Your persona has *OVERWHELMED* me.

I have *JOY* and *HAPPINESS* beyond description
because of you.

I *CHERISH* the intrigue of you.

You have *SOFTNESS* of skin and self that melts my heart.

Your *KINDNESS* and *THOUGHTFULNESS* add
a special dimension.

To your already *WARM* and *WONDERFUL* personality.

And I have fallen in *LOVE* with you more than all these.

WORDS can possibly say.

Daughter

At first she called me Daddy
Sweeter words I'd never known
They pulled at my heartstrings
Meant for me alone

Then she would say my father
How proud I was to hear
Simply adored that little girl
To my eyes she brought a tear

In all the intervening years
I've heard it o'er and o'er
I'll always cherish those words
Like I never heard them before.

There have been great moments
Through the good and the bad
One of the greatest was
When she called me Dad.

She'll always be my daughter
I'll always be her Dad
Just like my love is forever
A deeper love could not be had.

When I go on into eternity
Remember me with words of love
Tell the kids about old Gran'pa
I'll be waiting up above.

Son

He was only eight years old
Full of life and energy
Inquisitive
Positive
And as happy as could be

He was my firstborn
I was so proud of him
Curious
Compassionate
Love overflowed to the brim.

He was loving to his sisters
He looked after them
Caring
Protecting
Like a precious gem.

Then a car came careening by
He tried to cross the street
Disaster
Sorrow
His heart would no more beat.

We miss him every moment
And think of him daily
Remembrances
Reminiscences
Yet we recall his life gaily.

Farm Girl

I live in a little town
Not far from the farm
Few people live there
And none mean you harm

Each has his pickup truck
He drives it every day
Except on Sunday morning
Needless to say.

They farm both nuts and rice
Depending on the water
But I came not to farm
But to find the farmer's daughter

I own a pair of Levis
That's all I ever wear
They may get very dirty
But I know they'll never tear

Sometimes I want to dress up
And put on my very best
But this I must remember
I am away out West

So I'll just wear my brogans
And suspenders for my pants
Until I find that farm girl
And take her to the dance.

The Appliance Store

The refrigerator screamed
At the door,
"Close me, I'm empty,
There ain't no more."

The stove looked on
With anger and scorn
"I was a hot plate
When I was first born."

"I'm sunk," said the sink
The drain is clogged up
The disposal is broken
So Drain-O comes to disrupt

The washer and dryer were cozy at first
One always followed the other
But there finally came a day
When the dryer element began to wither

The dishwasher laughed
As it spit out the soap
Water pouring
All over the floor

The generator blew up
No heat or lights
So the alarm system
Just closed the store

Death Came Twice

Now I'm dead officially
Though the documents say I died this day
I really stopped living that early morning
May 27, 1967
It was in the small anteroom near the emergency ward
of an old run-down city hospital that I was told
my son would not have a ninth birthday
The doctors had done all that was possible
but the automobile that struck him caused too much
internal damage
His strong heart already had kept him alive for more than
six hours after the accident
but this was to be the end
The end of a dream
The end of me
My body functioned after that day
working
playing
fighting
loving
existing

as far as the rest of the world was concerned, but inside no
life stirred
It is only now that
mind
body
soul
are all at peace

Death this second time brought father and son together
Maybe I'll have a baseball player after all
but in the higher league, where there are no home runs
only a sacrifice

Love

Love

Love is an experience

An experience with another

Another that makes you think of no other

Love

Love is a feeling

A feeling that overwhelms you

Overwhelms to the point that nothing else matters

Love

Love is a force

A force that drives you

Drives you to unimaginable pleasures

Love

Love is a lifestyle

A lifestyle that says yes

Yes to all the wants and desires of someone else

Love

Love is a magnet

A magnet most powerful

Powerful enough to carry us into eternal bliss

Love

Love is a thought

A thought about you

You that fills mind and soul and spirit

Love

Love is life itself

A life that is complete

Complete joy and happiness, fulfillment, and contentment

What I Want

I want to take you to the movies
and go dancing
to walk the boardwalk hand in hand
go to a jazz festival

I want to sit with you on the sofa and watch TV
and go bike riding
to watch a sunset together
go to a baseball game

I want to drive the Pacific Coast Highway with you
and sit on a rocky ledge
to play a board game
go get an ice cream cone

I want to stare into those beautiful blue eyes
and lay on the beach
to say I love you
go on a cruise

I want to sit with a cup of coffee at the kitchen table with
you
and to hear you laugh
to take care of your hurts
go away with no place to go

I want to hold your hand when we cross the street
and feel your lips on mine
to catch you when you stumble
go to an antique show

I want to watch you when you sleep
and kiss the corners of your mouth
to make love to you when you awake
go through life with you

That's what I want.

A Life Fulfilled

If I should die today
not live another minute
my life would be complete
because of the time you were in it.

If I should die tomorrow
live for just a little while
my thoughts would always be of you
your lips, your touch, your smile.

If I should die ten years from now
and that time was spent with you
I'd be the richest man in the world
you've given me a heart brand new.

If I should live to be one hundred
and you're still by my side
such joy, such happiness, such pleasure
a lifetime roller coaster ride.

If I should live for all eternity
and have all joy and blessing too
nothing in that eon of time
would compare with loving you.

A Short Story

Starbucks at Four

Charlie had never been in a place like this. Everyone looked so young, which made him hesitate at the door for a moment. Cell phones, computers, iPods, and things Charlie could not identify were everywhere. Everywhere, that is, except at one table. That table was occupied by a middle-aged, gray-haired, well-dressed woman who immediately caught Charlie's eye. She looked up and smiled as he entered.

"May I?" Charlie queried, as he pointed to the empty chair at her table.

"Please—" she answered. Charlie excused himself to get a cup of coffee, offering also to get one for the woman. She declined and thanked him.

When Charlie turned from the counter with his coffee, planning to return to the table, the woman was gone. Had he offended her, he wondered. What did he do wrong? Was he too bold? What caused her to leave so abruptly? Pondering these and many more questions, Charlie removed his coat, worn against November chill, and sat alone at the table.

As he crossed his legs under the table to enjoy his coffee more comfortably, something fell to the floor. He retrieved a scrap of paper with the scribbled message: Starbucks at four. Was this for him, or was it there all morning, a note to someone else?

He started to crumple the note to throw it away; but then, he thought, maybe it *was* meant for him. The woman was certainly friendly, so he put the note in his pocket, finished his coffee, and left the table determined to be there at four o'clock the next day.

Charlie arrived about 30 minutes early the following day. At precisely four o'clock she walked in, spotted Charlie at the same table, and came over to sit across from him. "Hello, I'm Charlie."

"Yes, I know," she responded.

How could she know? I've never seen her before, and I certainly have never been in this place, he thought.

"I'm the girl of your dreams," she said, "and this meeting and your name were shown to me in one of *my* dreams." With no conversation, they shared coffee he bought in anticipation of their meeting.

Who is this woman, Charlie wondered, *and what does she want?* While his mind was in a whirl, she stood quickly, suggesting they go for a walk. Without thinking, Charlie followed this mysterious woman to the door, realizing that he felt, from his first look into her beautiful blue eyes and alluring smile the day before, that he knew her.

They walked to the far end of the parking lot where Charlie's car was parked and stood for a few minutes looking at one another. She abruptly kissed him, then turned, taking a few steps to her car. She got in and spoke through the open window. "Starbucks at four, my darling," she mouthed.

As she drove out of the parking lot, the word *darling* resounded in his ears, her soft sweet touch still on his hands, her sweet lips still fresh on his. Her car pulled onto the main street. Charlie's arm rose as if to stop the vehicle and pull it back to him. He heard his own voice, and without awareness of it happening, a scream: *Gawd, I love that woman!* He vowed he would pursue her with his thoughts.

> *One day we'll be together.*
> *One day we'll make love.*
> *One day we'll walk hand in hand.*

Other thoughts raced through Charlie's mind.

> *The journey has not been long enough.*
> *I don't want her to leave.*
> *Will I ever see her again?*

Then he remembered: Starbucks at four! But I don't even know her name!

That night Charlie dreamed that he met the shadowy woman with poetry in his heart, knowing that she was truly the girl of his dreams. In his dream, he took her into his arms, citing the words he had in his heart.

Let's go away to some far-off place
Where no one knows either you or me
We can sit and feel the salt air
With the sand between our toes.
Let's go away to a distant land
Far beyond what we could imagine
Balmy days and cool nights would engulf us
As we sit holding hands.

At four o'clock the next day (Charlie had been waiting since noon), she walked in and moved immediately to his table, then began telling him of her dream. It seems her dream paralleled his thoughts of yesterday and the poetry of his dream.

How did she know? he wondered. *Was this some cruel hoax someone was playing?* But Charlie was so overwhelmed by her he did not question.

Almost of one accord, they stood and headed for the exit. The words of the song: *April love is for the very young,* went through his mind. Charlie thought of this November love, as strange and one-sided as it seemed to be.

As they approached the door, Charlie turned to her, "Cynthia—!"

"Charlie," she responded.

How did he know? At that moment, each knew that this was meant to be, as unexplainable and as mysterious as it was.

Neither Charlie nor Cynthia went to Starbucks again; nor did they talk about or question those happenings on those three days.

Let it be!

Glimmerglass

An Indian summer day in the Adirondacks

Perfect for a cruise on the Glimmerglass Queen

The Hall of Fame

Fly Creek Mill

Cooper Museum

Twain study—all behind

The horn sounded and the bell clanged

We chugged toward the end of a 9-mile lake

Upstairs/Downstairs

Inside/Outside

The water

The view

The breeze

The sounds

A lighthouse

A campsite

An island

And the chug chug of a mighty engine

Mind drifts to simpler times

Bodies relaxed

Souls peaceful

A Familiar Short Story

Love: Simply

Bertha was nearly ninety-six years old when she died. In all that time, she had never said 'I love you' to anyone except the father of her five boys. Not to any of them—not to her subsequent three husbands—not to her nine sisters or one brother—not to anyone.

Bertha and Burt had been married a mere nine years when a logging accident took his life. What was she to do now? Five small sons. No husband. But Bertha was a survivor. Having been raised on a farm in Northern Minnesota she knew what hard work was all about.

No one ever did figure out how this plain, uneducated farm girl (she worked the fields with her only brother and the other men) could catch the town's most eligible bachelor. And he was quite handsome, too. But catch him she did.

It wasn't long before they had heeded the call to go West, ending up in a small town in Oregon, where the logging accident happened.

Bertha subsequently married a much older man who provided income and accepted those five small boys as his own.

Alfred was her middle son. Middle children always

seem to be the quirkiest, most impulsive, strong-willed, and just plain oddest of the group. Alfred was his own person, yet was very personable, energetic, and a hard worker. He excelled in school and became the only third Eagle Scout in that area, despite the limitations of the environment in which he lived: Poor and on the wrong side of the tracks, Alfred provided for himself with after-school and summer jobs.

His quick and deep mind, though, sometimes thought of relationships. Why didn't he have a best friend instead of just buddies and acquaintances? There were girls that he liked, but he never told them so. Why was that? He figured it was because he really didn't know how to say *it*—or even what to say. Mom never said *it*. The older brothers never talked about *it*. Maybe that was just the way it was.

A tour of duty in the military left Alfred on the East Coast. He never returned home. Marriage was, after all, the thing to do now. Settle down, get a job, and raise some kids. So that's what happened. Without fanfare, no lightning bolts into the heart, no walking on cloud nine, he just got married.

Fifty years, three children, five grandchildren, and two great-grandchildren later, Alfred was retired but quite healthy and energetic—as he always was. He had a little part-time job to keep busy—and to get out of the house, away from a wife that never seemed to be pleased with anything he did. Alfred was resigned to a life of empty and surface relationships, so, he was taken aback when a co-worker nearly seventeen years his junior befriended him. She seemed genuinely interested in what he was doing, what he was thinking, and how he was feeling. He, of course, couldn't tell her anything about feeling. Did he even have any feelings? If so, they were hidden away somewhere. But he did recognize that he was feeling something. Was it because of their conversations or just something in her life?

Alfred was intrigued. She brought something out of him. He liked that. He wanted to know more about her—and this feeling business. The thought suddenly crossed his mind: maybe in all of this, he would find out more about himself! But what was there to know? He was just an old man living out his days the best he could.

As the weeks and months passed, Alfred and Beth talked more and more. Finally, a luncheon date took place, phone calls were exchanged, e-mails were sent, and the bond between them strengthened.

Alfred thought often of her bright smile, beautiful brown eyes, lovely voice, but mostly he thought of the warmth of her being. He truly enjoyed being with her, and she seemed to reciprocate.

Could this be feelings? Alfred wondered. Is it possible

to have discovered them—that he really did have some—after all this time? *Can someone have feelings for me?* He dismissed the thought as quickly as it appeared.

Several days later, as Alfred and Beth were lunching together, their hands accidentally touched across the table. Neither moved; their eyes met. Still, no one moved or looked away. An eternity seemed to pass. Simultaneously, they smiled. The waitress brought the coffee and the world around them was restored. But from that day on, something *felt* different.

In the days following, Alfred thought often of that moment when their hands touched, and their eyes met. It gave him a wonderful feeling inside. *Feeling?* Maybe so. But no, certainly someone like Beth could not have any thoughts of him except as a friendly old man who worked alongside her. *Or could she?* That memory gave Alfred many pleasant evenings despite the drone of his wife's voice and endless chatter about nothing.

At the company picnic several months later, Alfred and Beth were enjoying the warm sun and picnic fare of hot dogs and salads. They sat on a blanket under a large oak tree away from the crowd.

Alfred broke the silence, surprising even himself. "You know," he said to Beth, "I really like you. I don't want to complicate things or make you uncomfortable or create a situation with any repercussions," he blurted, "but I think a lot of you. I hope I'm not out of bounds," he added shyly.

As he dropped his eyes in embarrassment at what he'd just said, Alfred saw a slight smile appear on his lunch partner's face.

"And I like you," she whispered quietly.

Nothing more was said. The picnic ended, and they exchanged goodbyes.

And I like you, reverberated through Alfred's mind again and again during the following days. *Was this feeling?* he wondered.

Beth went on a week-long vacation the day after the picnic, so Alfred hadn't seen or spoken with her since that day. Three days later, he decided to check his e-mail, though not expecting anything since Beth was gone and only she sent him messages. When Alfred opened his e-mail and read the few words on the screen (four exactly with her name), they triggered and released a gamut of emotions. "Oh, my God," Alfred shouted to the empty house. He repeated it several times, jumping to his feet and knocking the chair backward. His heart pounded in his chest, and he began giggling uncontrollably. Then he laughed until laughter turned to sobs. Tears streaked his cheeks.

"Oh, my God," he repeated. "It's true, it's really true."

The cycle repeated—joyous laughter, sobbing, a

feeling of disbelief cast aside by secure knowledge and understanding of the words he had read.

Alfred glanced out the window, not looking for anything in particular; he paced through the house, stared at the words on the screen, and finally sat in the upright chair. A sense of calm settled over him as he spoke the words inside his head: After all these years, now I know.

Alfred looked again at the message and read it aloud:

I love you, simply.

Beth

Chic

She's a downtown woman
with an uptown smile
though her heart is in the country
she is always right in style.

She goes out dancing in Harlem
she buys her clothes in Queens
now she dines at Sardis
but she was raised on pork and beans.

She often dreams of yesterday
and thinks about her family
but she won't give up her life today
to return to the way it used to be.

Miss You

What does it mean to miss you?

It means to have a hole in my heart, to have emptiness in
my soul.

What does it mean to miss you?

It means not to feel your lips on mine, to not have your
arms around me.

What does it mean to miss you?

It means to have a longing for your presence, to desire
looking deeply into your eyes.

What does it mean to miss you?

It means to want you near me always, to want our bodies
meshed as one.

What does it mean to miss you?

It means to desire knowing all about you, to share feelings,
hurts, and desires.

What does it mean to miss you?

It means wanting you near me that I might protect you, to
want to spend our lives

together.

The NASCAR Nag

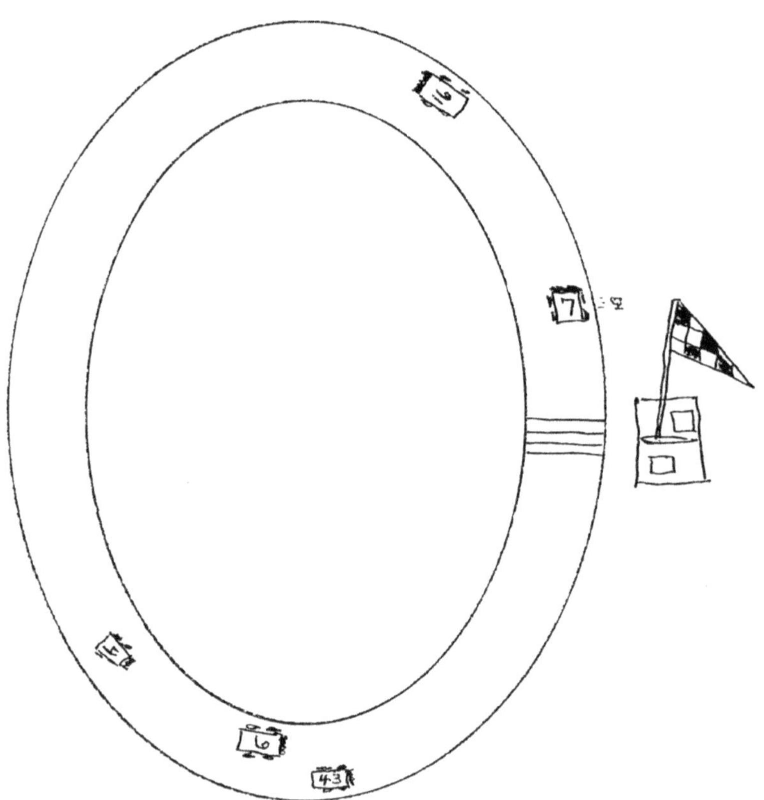

An Ironic Short Story

Vs.
Versus: against, in contrast to

It all started so innocently. Just being young, and a boy. Fights that ended with a black eye and a bloody nose. Usually, his. But as Frank got older, battles became more frequent and more furious. There was something or someone inside him that clouded his judgment, made him angry, pushed him to the edge, and created a deep desire within toward confrontations.

This new relationship, though, seemed different. Frank stood there beside his car as she drove out of the parking lot with the word 'darling' resounding in his ears, her soft touch still felt on his hand, her moist, sweet lips fresh on his. As her car pulled onto the main street, Frank's arm raised as if to stop it and pull her back. Without an awareness of it happening, Frank's voice screamed, "I love that woman."

He remembered words he'd written days earlier . . .

My darling, I write these words
today from a heart ready to burst.
A heart not broken but exploding with desire.
Desire to know you more fully.
Desire to experience you more completely.
Desire that words cannot express!

Never in Frank's life had he felt like this. He hoped that feeling would last forever. Little did he know it was about to change in a way he could never imagine.

Frank and Sophie had been seeing each other for several months. They were both in unhappy and troubled marriages. Their bond started as friendship but grew into a close and loving relationship, and now, Frank did not want to let her go. She, however, seemed content to leave things as they were. He wanted her all to himself, but that meant getting rid of her husband and leaving his wife, who he was sure, was seeing someone else anyway.

That old desire for confrontation welled up inside Frank, directed at his wife and Sophie's husband. Frank decided he needed a plan. A plan that would result in quenching the fires within: the fire of anger and the fire of desire.

Then, an epiphany roared in: Eliminate *him,* meaning Sophie's husband, and he would have *her,* meaning Sophie, thought Frank. My wife wants to leave anyway, he reasoned; but the plan must be foolproof. No mistakes. No miscalculations.

Sophie told Frank that her husband went bowling every Friday night. That's how they could be together. Frank's wife had her bridge games on Fridays. A plan started to fester.

Perfect, he breathed.

At least, he hoped it would be perfect. Not like a few months earlier when Frank vowed to get even with a driver who cut him off at an intersection. He followed the driver, at a distance, to his home and planned a face-to-face. A few days later, he put the vengeful plan into action.

Frank sat in the neighborhood bar all afternoon, consuming beer after beer and mentally going over the night's schedule. When the hour came, he got into his car and drove toward the house of his anticipated victim.

Parking a few blocks away, Frank crept up to the porch, ignited a small fire, and banged on the door. When the occupant, the errant driver, came out of the house, Frank grabbed him and would not let him go. "See how it feels to be unable to go where you want and need to go?" Frank screamed into the man's face. "I wanted to get through that intersection, and you wouldn't let me!"

Before Frank could say more, a cruising police officer saw the flames, grabbed an extinguisher from his patrol car, and doused the fire. Assuming Frank was an alcoholic, the officer subsequently arrested him and placed him in a rehab facility. Frank was stripped of everything but his most necessary clothing during his stay. He had a cigarette smuggled in, but the problem was he had no matches. For the next several days, he tried any means to light the cigarette, from making a spark with two metal objects to pressing it against a light bulb.

Nothing had worked. His plan had gone awry from the beginning.

What made him think his new plan in securing his union with Sophie would work, then? It had to.

Pondering his present dilemma, Frank vowed that this time there would be no drinking. A clear mind would prevail. But how could the removal of Sophie's husband be accomplished?

Before Frank could think about the problem any longer, an answer came. His wife announced at dinner that they were going on a cruise. Frank's first thought was that accidents do happen on cruises. *Perfect, indeed,* he mused.

Another epiphany: Tell Sophie to make plans for the same cruise. It may be a cliché, but the old adage—kill two birds with one stone—popped into Frank's mind. *Better than perfect* came from his lips as they curled in anticipation.

Sophie agreed to his plan, and everything was set.

On embarkation day, as Frank and his wife boarded via the gangplank, Frank saw Sophie and her husband already on the ship, watching from the upper deck. Frank and Sophie's eyes met, and they sensed what the next few days were to bring.

At dinner that evening, the first night out, Frank and his wife were being escorted to their table when in the distance, there again was Sophie. The maitre'd was walking straight toward her. *Could this be?* Yes, they were seated at the same table! How convenient.

Waiting until they were seated, Sophie spoke, "Hi, I'm Sophie. My husband will be back shortly." Not a sign of recognition showed on either Frank or Sophie's faces that they knew each other.

Sophie's husband returned, and more introductions were made. A bit of awkwardness seemed to prevail, but all concerned were cordial. The meal was finished, and goodnight greetings were conveyed.

Then, on the third night out, Frank was sitting alone on deck when a figure approached. He could not see the person's face, but he recognized the special-order hooded (and expensive) windbreaker he had purchased for his wife, especially for this cruise. He dashed behind the lifeboats, hiding from any passersby.

The figure stopped right in front of where Frank was concealed; she leaned on the rail and looked out over the moonlit water. He knew this was the awaited opportunity. He would take care of the husband at another time.

He crept from his hiding place, quietly approached the figure, and grabbing her around the waist, pushed her overboard. At the last second, the woman turned her face toward him, the jacket hood fell back, and Sophie's horrified face stared back at him.

"Oh, my God, what have I done?" screamed Frank, as Sophie disappeared into the churning dark water below. Unbeknownst to Frank, Sophie had borrowed the windbreaker from his wife earlier in the evening. Sophie always did like expensive things.

Dazed, Frank headed back to his cabin. Approaching the door, he heard voices inside.

"Now that that's done, we can be together," Frank heard his wife say.

Sophie's husband replied, "And it was so easy!"

The NASCAR Nag

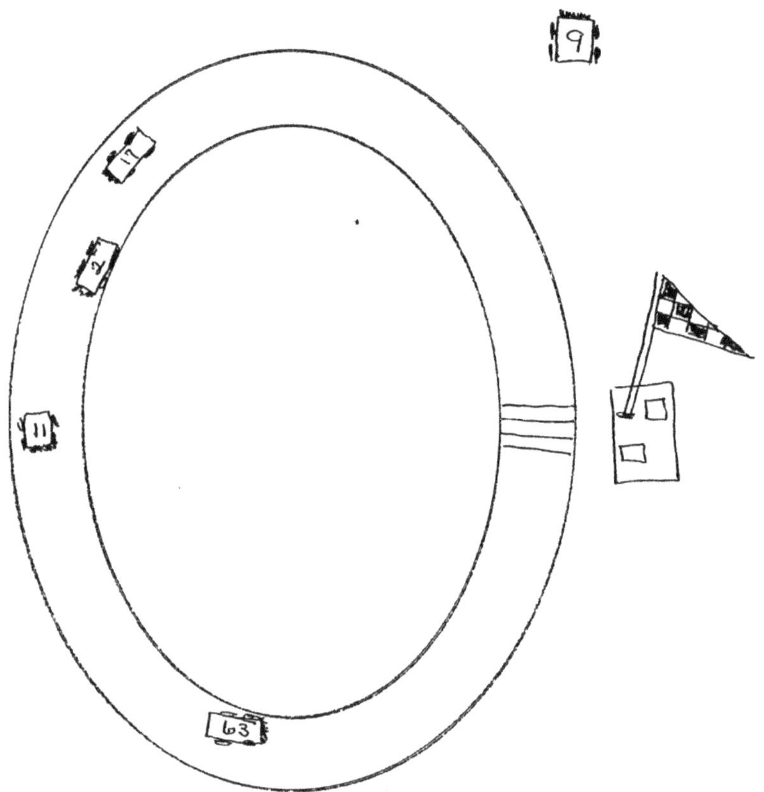

A Medium Short Story

Lost and Found

It was six o'clock when the *Alisa Lee* pulled away from the dock. Captain Al had made all the necessary checks—the motor was running smoothly, the tag line was removed and thrown back onto the pier, and he felt as if he was ready to go. Al knew it was a long trip—perhaps too long for someone alone—but he was confident that the love of his life (the *Alisa Lee*) was up to the task.

As the fog began to lift, Al looked at his watch—exactly 6:00 a.m. He pushed the throttle forward. The water churned behind the long, sleek beauty Al cherished, and the journey began, a journey that would involve feelings and emotions, fears and joys, and moments of decision that he had never faced before.

With all the windows open and the wind blowing briskly in his face, Al stood in the wheelhouse with a feeling of freedom and exhilaration. He watched the shoreline slowly disappear in the distance. Now with nothing but water all around, Al kept the *Alisa Lee* in a steady south-by-southwest direction. His calculations told him that would take him to his destination in approximately thirty-two hours, barring any unforeseen circumstances. And, unforeseen they were.

At 12:45 p.m., Al left the bridge with the wheel secured and the compass telling him that he was right on course. Hunger pangs had overtaken him suddenly, so he headed below to see what the galley had to offer. He had stocked it himself but couldn't quite remember all that he had brought aboard. After looking through the cupboard and refrigerator, he settled on a ham and cheese sandwich, some chips, and a soda.

That'll hold me for a while, Al mused aloud.

Twenty minutes later, the lunch was gone so he headed topside. When he got to the bridge, he thought something was amiss. The boat seemed to be going in the wrong direction. He noticed the sun behind him instead of on the starboard side where it should have been. The wheel was still secured as he'd left it—the compass still read SSW—but something was wrong!

Maybe I should turn back, Al thought—*but how can I, when I don't know which direction is "back"?* The wind was coming from the wrong direction (or so it seemed), the sun was in the wrong place, the compass had gone crazy, and his nautical skills had gone awry.

Don't panic—Al remembered his many hours traversing the waters that now seemed utterly foreign to him.

Stop and think, came to his mind. *Be calm.*

Then, just as he began to ingest and process these thoughts, a loud sound came from under the boat near the bow. Al wondered if he'd hit something, so he immediately went forward and looked over the side near where the anchor was attached.

Nothing there, no visible damage. When Al thought of possible damage to his beautiful *Alisa Lee*, his mind flashed back to another time. Another time when his heart burned at the thought or sight of the woman he truly loved.

She had disappointed him and left suddenly, leaving damage to his feelings seemingly beyond repair. But don't let the *beyond repair* happen again. Al thought he had left all that behind. But here it was!

No turning back.

Suddenly, the vessel lurched and turned sharply to the left. Al was sure he had hit something, and whatever it was forced him to turn. As he grabbed the wheel (even though it was still secured), Al glanced at the compass. It still read SSW!

But we turned, Al reasoned. *What as going wrong? I've got to get under there and see what's going on.*

Donning scuba gear, Captain Al got ready to submerge. What he found would change his life completely and profoundly.

A girl, clinging to the rudder, was steering the ship. She smiled and beckoned him to come closer. This had to be a dream. Maybe he had bumped his head when the ship lurched and this was all a fantasy, a figment of his imagination.

But he could not resist her charms. Responding to her gestures, he swam toward her. As he got closer, he realized who it was, the one who had broken his heart so long ago. And there she was.

No, no, he thought, *I can't do this again.*

He was helpless as she pulled him toward her like a magnet. Just as he was within arm's reach, she suddenly darted away.

He let her go. Her parting words would remain seared in his mind for years to come. But then, just as now, at the last moment, as her *I love you* faded away, he knew he would never see her again. How wrong he was!

Al gathered his thoughts, concluding it was all an illusion. He examined the craft and surfaced, finding everything in working order. Discarding the wet suit and stowing the scuba equipment, he went to the cabin.

The craft righted itself, the sun was where it was supposed to be, the compass was correct, and all seemed right with the world. But Al could not get the experience of the girl out of his mind. What did it mean? Surely something. She had pulled the same stunt when she dumped him. Teasing and enticing him to come along—then smash! He could not shake her from him even though reality made him realize that what had just happened was not real.

With the boat secured again, Al dropped to his bunk for a quick nap. He soon fell into a deep sleep. Awaking with a start, after only a few minutes of rest, Al saw that it was dark. He'd been asleep for several hours. He immediately checked the instruments, and all seemed to be in order. They were headed in the right direction.

A few hours later, he spotted land. There, on the shore, was a beautiful nymph of a woman waving furiously. Al was again drawn to thoughts of several years ago.

She had broken his heart twice before. Was this a precursor of what was ahead?

Could he break the spell? Just turn and run (or sail, as the case may be). But he could not! Again, he was drawn toward her. As he got close, he saw that she was barely covered and wrapped only with seaweed.

He remembered the many days and nights spent together. Not only their bodies, but their lives enmeshed in one another. Her soft body, beautiful words, tender touch—oh, how he had loved her.

But then, she had once again pulled out of his life with nary a word. Is that what she was doing now in his imagination? Or was it genuinely real? *What does she want? What is my response supposed to be?*

That's it! thought Al. I must find the key to all that is happening. No turning back!

Al contemplated: the rudder—that's it. He must right the wrong, get going in the right direction—and don't run away; the bump—understand the circumstances of why; the shore—abandoned but not forgotten. Could this be the answer? *I have to find out.*

He turned slightly toward where the nymph-like creature was situated on shore. Quickly running the boat ashore, Al jumped out and ran toward where she had been. Catching a glimpse of her, he quickened his pace. He caught up to her about 60 yards down the white, sandy beach.

She turned away, but Al held her face toward him, cupping her chin. *It was her! Now what?*

Holding tightly to her arm so as not to let her slip away, he stared into her beautiful blue eyes. She must have read his heart like an open book. She was who he really wanted. And most certainly he was who she had wanted.

Without a word spoken, they slowly walked hand in hand down the pure white sandy beach. No turning back and never letting go. Al thought all was well, a happy ending—peace and contentment at last. As it should be.

That was before *it* happened.

When they got back to where Al had run ashore, there was nothing. *Alisa Lee* was gone. There was not even any evidence of her ever having been there. He loosened his grip on the girl's arm, and before he realized it, the nymph had vanished. Both loves of his life had disappeared, back to the sea.

Al's heart ached at that realization. Not knowing what else to do, he began trudging up the beach, looking for a clue to explain, at the very least, the *Alisa Lee's* disappearance.

An hour passed. The captain was tired. Sitting on a log that had washed up on the shore, Al tried to think. But his mind went to *Alisa Lee* and the woman he had named her for.

The experience with the boat paralleled the time with the girl. Up, down, up, down. Good, bad, good, bad. What was he to do now? Getting drowsy, he sat on the sand and rested his head on the log. It was not long before he fell fast asleep.

He awoke with a start. Taking a few minutes to orient himself, Al glanced one way and then the other. Nothing there. Subconsciously, he then looked out to the sea.

What was that? It looked like a boat—similar to the *Alisa Lee*. Was there someone on the deck? As the image neared, he recognized it. Both of his loves had returned to him—the boat and the girl.

Al jumped into the water, and half ran, half swam toward the vessel. Upon reaching *Alisa Lee*, he climbed aboard, and fell into the arms of his true love. He grabbed the spinning wheel of the helm and turned back to sea. And the girl twined around him. Now, truly, there would be no turning back.

Without warning, as if on cue, the girl wrestled out of his arms, ran to the aft deck, and threw herself overboard.

Oh, no—not again! Al screamed. He let go of the wheel, causing the boat to turn sideways and run amok as he tried to throw her a lifeline.

She purposely avoided the line and plunged beneath the white foam of the open water. The boat lurched one last time, causing Al to fall and everything went dark.

When Al awoke, he found himself on the open ledge of a rocky cliff. Below, he saw the remains of the *Alisa Lee*, her mast broken and split and sheared boards of her hull floating away. It broke his heart to see her in such disarray. Was there any way of saving her now? As in life, the sea would have its way—up, down, up down—joy, sadness, despair, euphoria. *How many times must he go through this?*

Third time a charm? Bullshit! Al dejectedly stumbled to the wreckage. Recognizing what had been the stern, he climbed onto the devastation that had once been his pride and joy, his eternal love.

No! he shouted aloud to an empty beach. *This cannot be the end.* He had plans. *I can't quit now,* Al thought. Didn't I have a goal to reach? Did I not say *No Turning Back*?

Mustering all his strength and will and fortitude, he began to salvage what was left of his beloved *Alisa Lee*. Out of the splintered planks and twisted metal, Al fashioned a raft. *You may not look like the original, but you will soon be sea-worthy again,* he vowed to her.

As Al diligently put together a craft upon which he hoped he would be able to continue his journey, his mind turned to the sea nymph that disappeared as quickly as she had appeared. *What was all that about? Vanished—just like that!* Maybe she would return when the raft, *Alisa Lee II*, was put to sea. Those thoughts, and those of his tortured lost loves, kept his mind on the job ahead.

Six long and exhausting days later, kept alive by gnawing seaweed and suckling strange fruit he found growing nearby, he salvaged enough material from the wreck, and the raft was complete.

Let's hope she'll stay afloat, Al muttered. *I'll head her west toward the sunset.* The makeshift sail replaced the mighty engine that had powered the *Alisa Lee* just a few days earlier, but Al was satisfied with the results of his efforts. *Westward, Ho!* he shouted.

Barely two days at sea, Al spotted another object off the raft's port side. Al maneuvered the tiny but sturdy craft toward the bobbing thing. Within sight, He could not believe his eyes. It was the *Alisa Lee!* And she looked beautiful. Intact. *But how could that be?*

Al steered his homemade raft up to the boat, abandoned the raft, and climbed aboard. There in the wheelhouse was the nymph, the love he had desired and cherished.

In his excitement and anxiety, as he lurched forward, Al caught his foot in ropes coiled on deck. He stumbled, hitting his head on a large metal storage box, and again the world went dark.

Much later, upon opening his eyes, Al found himself in the hospital with a beautiful girl by his side. The woman was her, his love! "What? How?" he stammered.

"Rest," she said, "We'll talk later."

The next day she began her story. "When you left, I finally realized I did not want you to go. So, I rented a boat and operator and searched for you. I found the *Alisa Lee,* grounded but undamaged, and you on the beach's edge, unconscious and suffering from sunstroke. We packed you in ice and brought you to the hospital. You've been gone for almost two weeks."

Al stammered, "What about the wreck, the raft, the nymph, the compass?" He noticed everyone in the room exchanging glances. "And the seaweed?" Al insisted. "It is only found at extreme depths where no one could survive without proper gear."

Did they think he was delirious, maybe? Al thought for a moment. No, he was not imagining things—just looking for a love that evaded him for so long. *I knew I'd find it if I looked, no matter what.*

And he did.

No turning back!

The NASCAR Nag

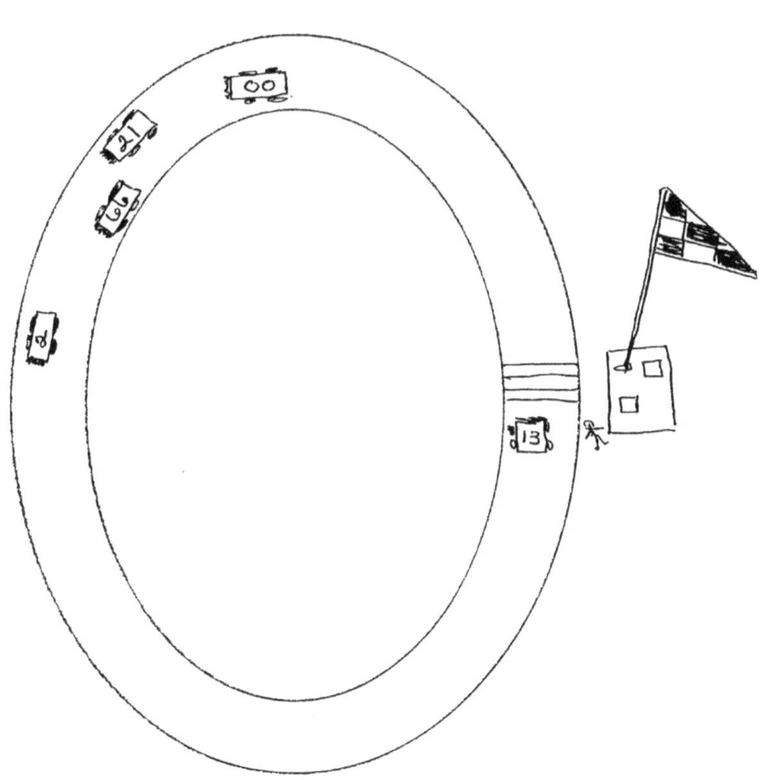

Yellow Butterflies

I was sitting on the porch
thinking of you
when two yellow butterflies
came into view.
They flitted around each other,
perhaps in love.
I thought of us
and our blessings from above.
Was there some meaning
for that meeting today?
The butterflies smiled
enjoying their foray.
God smiled
when he put us together.
It was His will, I am sure.
He meant for us to meet
and for our love to endure.
I love you my darling
as the butterflies can attest
I am yours for always;
in that promise
you can rest.

Bookcase

It's not only a bookcase to hold and display books or, perhaps knick-knacks, but it is also a piece of furniture made of beautiful, expensive wood, polished to a sheen. It has four glass-paneled doors with ring-type handles and sits majestically across the room from the sofa on which I sit. Every shelf is filled with books, magazines, pamphlets, and other reading material.

How wonderful it would be if I could travel from book to book, shelf by shelf as a character in or witness to the adventures these books hold. There would be a grand tour across this great land we call America. I would be a companion of the Apostle Paul journeying to Rome, where he was imprisoned and spent time writing his letters to new churches he'd established. I could be a witness with the prophet Jeremiah as he trudged from place-to-place warning of devastation to come.

There I'd be in the trenches at Normandy battling for freedom; I see myself in a large leather chair consoling those with emotional and psychological problems; or, as co-author with literary greats of bygone days; playing bridge with and against the genius minds of past centuries; shaping and rebuilding minds with knowledge beyond my imagination.

As I look at the bookcase from a larger perspective, I find myself in a *what-if* mood. I cannot go back in time or place (though that might be my *druthers*); but what-if I had done this instead of that, gone here instead of there, said yes instead of no—and so many other choices. But I am here. This is now. I must determine to do the best for the most, according to my abilities and talents.

In *that* I find solace.

The bookcase is still there. It looks the same and contains the same books, magazines, and brochures. But I cannot concentrate on what the reading material contains. Something or someone is making my mind jump from book to book, shelf to shelf, in no apparent sequence. It seems as if I don't care about what's inside those book covers.

The red-jacketed books have an eerie glow, almost fluid-like. Others change shape as I stare at them. I never noticed before, but most of them are lying on their sides instead of standing upright.

Did someone change their position from two days ago? Why can't I focus? What's going on in the recesses of my mind? Why am I now drawn to Robert Bly's *Iron John*?

As a tear rolls down my cheek, my eyes turn to Jeremiah, the so-called *Weeping Prophet*. Why and for whom am *I* weeping? I don't think I can write any more.

Something inside says: Go and tell! Go where? Tell what?

Perhaps night will answer the questions and relieve the uneasiness inside me.

If I can sleep.

Sleep.

The Pearl-Handled Knife

I was only seven and my brother was six.
We came home from school and got in a fix.
We stoked the wood fire, it blazed and blazed.
The chimney was cracked, the house was razed.

Hidden in a nook in the wall with care
was my pearl-handled knife I'd won at the fair.
When the ashes cooled, I searched and sought,
I looked for hours but all was for naught.

More than fifty years later I told this tale,
Of my pearl-handled knife and my travail
I related the story while pastoring a church,
and that would set off a frantic search.

I spent many years in the service of our Lord,
not looking for glory not looking for reward.
What I did receive was better than gold
It was love—more than tenfold.

After retirement I returned as a guest
To speak about missions and let God do the rest.
When the service concluded I was presented a gift,
A pearl-handled knife! —an emotional lift.

Today I treasure my pearl-handled knife.
And am grateful to God for an abundant life.
I'll never forget my thoughtful friends.
True love continues—it never ends.

Prose about Snows

As the snow began to fall in the forest
all the animals, large and small, scurried for shelter
old man winter was on his way.

It was time to put away what was needed
for the long cold nights and hope it lasted
until the thaw of the first Spring day.

Atop the highest mountain peak the snow
had already fallen several inches
and was topped with an icy crust.

Along the slopes the drifts began to pile
as the tree limbs were forced to the ground
but they held under the strain as they must.

But beneath the severity of the elements
were many cozy nests that were built
knowing of the days that were to come.

So let the cruel winds heartily blow
and let the icy patches form above
mighty God has provided a home for all.

A Lonely Man

Do you know the heart of a lonely man?
Do you know the emptiness he feels?
He sits alone in the restaurant,
parts of the lives from others he steals.

He wants to love and be loved
but most do not know he is alone.
From outside he looks quite happy,
so the longing to be needed he will condone.

The NASCAR Nag

"I said "You turn"—not U-turn"

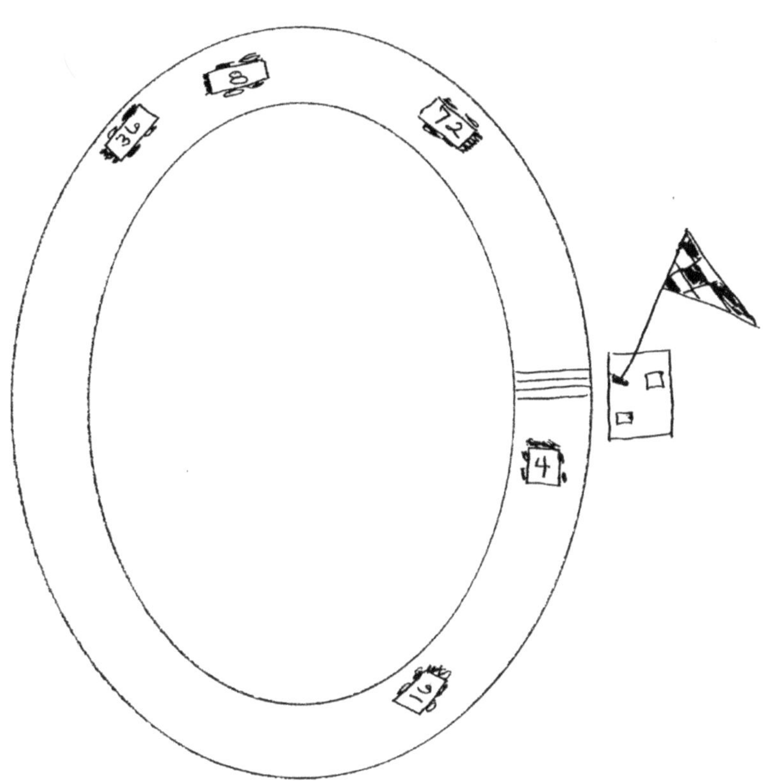

A Trilogy Short Story

I: The Miracle of Romance

II: The Security of Commitment

III: The Cruelty of Revenge

1: The Miracle of Romance

The luxury liner pulled into the designated spot for disembarking the passengers. Among those passengers was a six-year-old girl brought up in the lap of high society and wealth. Alongside the gargantuan ship was a freighter, designated for cargo, but a few passengers were aboard. Among those passengers was an infant boy. As both ships disembarked passengers, the girl glanced toward the freighter, and her eyes rested on the infant child of apparent refugees, crew members, or stowaways. The baby squealed, and their eyes met. The girl did not understand the feeling that the moment gave her. She was, after all, just six years old. But she would never forget.

Hannah was now thirty-seven and very successful in her own right; that is, she did not need her parents' money or positions to succeed. She had remained single and was very happy and content with her life, in spite of the constant subtleties about marriage and family.

Robert, at age thirty-one, was still struggling. He had finished college but could not find a position or employment that suited him or his talents. Even his love life seemed stalled. Whichever girl, he'd tell himself, *she just isn't the right one.*

An employer new in town was advertising for engineers. Right up my alley, Robert thought excitedly. Maybe this is my chance.

Robert's initial interview was followed by training in Philadelphia. He secured the position and began his career on a positive note. His first day on the job, he was introduced to his co-worker, who had been with the company for a number of years. And had a Ph.D.! This intimidated Robert somewhat. But his fear dissipated at their first formal meeting.

Hannah, this is Robert, Robert, Hannah. You two will be working together.

After several months, Robert and Hannah began seeing each other outside of work. Those lunch and coffee dates eventually turned into serious romance. Robert and Hannah began sharing their life experiences on one of those dates. Each told childhood tales. When it got to the point of telling how they had each reached New York, they discovered they had both arrived on the same day. They were the ones who had exchanged glances during disembarkation.

Since Robert was an infant, he had no recollection of the incident. Hannah, on the other hand, fully recalled the experience.

The phrase, *Meant to be,* gained new meaning and solidified their feelings and commitment to one another.

11: The Security Of Commitment

Paula had never flown before, but she decided to go this one time by plane. So, she boarded the plane, filled with trepidation and nervousness.

Some of those fears were diminished when she discovered that her seat was next to an older, very handsome man. He smiled pleasantly as she squeezed into her seat. They were in first-class but because he was seated on the aisle, she still had to somewhat step over him. She apologized; he smiled again.

Once Paula was settled, she felt more comfortable and relaxed. They engaged in pleasant conversation and discovered that they were both headed for the same destination.

This coincidence frightened Paula. She feared running into him, which seemed likely, in the small village where they were headed. What would she say? Once outside the plane, she knew her shyness and insecurity would show through.

At long last, Richard relaxed. He was going home. Home. To that little cottage by the lake. Away from the hustle and bustle of the city. Home, where the only noise was the tiny waves breaking on the shore. And perhaps the chirping of a bird or two somewhere out there.

Richard had hurried most of his life: business, social obligations, children, wife (until her passing a few months earlier), investments, money management, trips back and forth from the city to the cabin—which consisted of entertaining clients—and endless meetings. Now was the time to unwind. The business was sold. No more commitments, just my time, Robert mused.

The company's 100th Anniversary party was bound to be a success. Good food, music, awards, dancing, special speakers, and honored guests.

Paula was initially hesitant about going. Being a relatively new employee, she hardly knew anyone, and a huge crowd would always make her uncomfortable.

Richard, likewise, was dubious about going to the celebration. He was invited as the main speaker, so he felt obligated to go. He'd spent thirty-six years working and traveling for them—so the least he could do was attend and receive the deserved adulation.

He did not look forward to meeting the new people. All of them gushing over his successes gets tiresome, Richard thought, as he rehearsed answers to potential questions.

Paula hesitantly seated herself at her assigned spot (four to a table) and waited for the main speaker.

When he appeared from the side (stage left, that is), Paula was shocked to see the speaker was her seatmate on the plane.

Finishing up, Richard left the speaker's platform and headed straight for Paula's table. There was an empty chair, and he immediately seated himself there.

Hello, I'm Richard, he announced, looking straight at Paula.

Yes, she responded, I know.

To the quizzical look on his face, Paula quickly added—from the airplane, remember?

Of course, I remember—Paula, right?

From that exchange, a long-lasting relationship began; most of the many years were spent together at that cottage by the lake.

Business behind.

Shyness gone.

And a love made for the centuries.

III: The Cruelty of Revenge

Bonnie was barely eight years old when (she thought) she was in love with her older sister's boyfriend.

Someday, she schemed, someday.

Days, weeks, months, years went by. Relationships came and went, but Bonnie never forgot.

Ken had been transferred to the office downtown, which, in turn, necessitated a move. He packed everything and rented a flat not far from the studio (he was an artist and musician). Though he did not like the urban setting, it suited his present needs.

Every time Bonnie passed a man on the street she would think, *Is that him? It's been many years and I know he's matured—but it could be him! No—too short, too tall, wrong eye color, etc.* This scenario happened again and again. It began to overwhelm her to the point of mania. It affected her very existence and function as a productive member of society.

She dared not share this with anyone. They would surely think she was losing her mind. Still, those words from long ago haunted her—someday, someday.

That someday came when Bonnie was sitting at the neighborhood bar sipping a Margarita. Another patron summoned the bartender who answered, calling him by name. *That's him! That's my Ken,* Bonnie realized.

Bonnie stayed at the bar until Ken left. He hailed a cab—she did, too, and followed him. Now I know where he lives. I can make my plans. This is someday.

Ken's day had been long and exhausting. Multiple trips from his new apartment to his former office to clear up left over strings or loose ends. The short stop at the local tavern and a quick beer had settled him down a bit. Now, off to home.

Three days later, things began to get crazy. Ken could not understand what was going on. First, two flat tires. Then, phone calls from no one, just laughter from the receiver, emails from an unknown sender, knocks on the door at midnight, and love letters with no return address or signature inside.

Eventually, those incidents turned into threats on Ken's life. That's when he called the police. Their response: We can't do anything until a crime is committed. But we will monitor your phone to see if we can locate the perpetrator.

Three weeks into that madness, as Ken was at the market, he got the feeling he was being watched. One woman in particular seemed to be everywhere he was. She even winked at him. Then she rammed her cart into his. Ken got out of there as quickly as possible.

By that time, Bonnie was excited beyond words, but

that was not enough. She needed the *coup-de-grâce*.

This was it. She called Ken on the phone, and when he answered, Bonnie told him she was his nemesis. She told him to meet her at 2:00 a.m. the following day at an old, deteriorating apartment complex. Unbeknownst to Ken, this was the building where Bonnie and her sister lived while growing up.

She promised to explain everything, and she let him know of her love for him all these years.

Ken knew the only way to stop the madness was to go, and he did, though reluctant and frightened.

When he arrived at the dilapidated old building, Bonnie was standing at the fourth-floor broken window. She motioned for him to come up. As he went in looking for a stairway, Ken thought: *Who is this woman, and what does she want?* At the fourth-floor landing, Bonnie appeared from the room where she'd been standing.

Remember me? Bonnie asked. Or perhaps you remember my sister. Why didn't you love me the way you loved my sister? I've suffered all these years, so now it's your turn.

Ken responded. What are you talking about? I don't know you or your sister. What do you want?

Don't get coy with me, Bonnie said. I've suffered all these years loving you, and now it's payback time. She pulled a large knife from under her clothes and advanced toward Ken.

When she lurched at him, Ken jumped aside, grabbing the knife by the blade. It cut deeply; blood spurted everywhere.

Bonnie threw the knife aside when Ken relaxed his grip and Ken picked it up, thinking only of escape.

Now! Bonnie screamed. Everyone will think you pushed me out the window as I tried to get away. Your fingerprints are on the murder weapon. You'll spend the rest of your life remembering that this could have been avoided—simply by loving me.

Suddenly, she ran toward the window and flung herself out.

The small group of long-time friends sat at the table waiting for dinner. Conversation turned to the closeness of the group and the wonder of how long they had been together. The same five people: Hannah and Robert, Paula and Richard, and Ken. Even after losing his wife to cancer, he continued to meet with his friends. But this night, one was missing.

Has Ken a new lady friend? one of the others inquired. That's what I heard.

No, they were told, he simply was mistaken for someone else.

The Cedar Box

Downstairs where boxes are stored
is a trunk
not opened for many years.
Inside the trunk is a cedar box.
I'd thought about it from time to time.
Now I must go see.

It stared back, daring me to open it.
I knew what was inside:
a baseball glove
second-grade homework papers,
pajamas.

It stared back
Daring me to expose my emotions
I knew what they were:
Anger
Regret
Loss.

It stared back
the lid already ajar; I knew I had to look:
a Father's Day card
photograph with his sisters
Christmas stocking.

It stared back
drawing me nearer, I knew I could not retreat:
sadness

fear

emptiness.

It stared back
I boldly walked forward and jerked open the lid
there it all was
pictures and drawings once taped to the refrigerator
baby book
Orioles' banner and Baltimore Colts' picture
Birth certificate
winter cap
pictures of my father, his grandfather
homework dated 5/26/67
first-grade report card
I held onto the memories
never to fear the cedar box again.

Another Short Story

The Dog Lady

(Warning to dog owners: Do not read)

Everyone in the neighborhood knew Miss Pritchard, calling her the dog lady since she talked endlessly about her little 'Muffin'. Strangely, though, no one had ever seen Muffin. Some thought the dog was imaginary, while others thought she was just very protective of her pet. After all, the two of them lived in a very large house. Perhaps Muffin had a room of her own. Miss Pritchard was quite eccentric, and she clearly loved that dog, as she often told others.

Not only did she love her own pet, but she asked everyone, especially children, to bring her strays or unwanted dogs that she could care for and eventually find them homes. She would only take small dogs. She preferred Toy Poodles, Pomeranians, Maltese terriers, Shih Tzu, Pekinese, Bichon Friese, and the like. Many were brought to her; and apparently, they were well cared for and placed in new homes because they were never seen in the neighborhood again. Miss Pritchard purchased only the best dog food in quantities far beyond the amount her sweet Muffin could consume.

Patty Ann and Charlie were very inquisitive twelve-year-olds. They decided they had listened to Miss Pritchard go on and on about that dog of hers for the last time. They wanted to see Muffin. Whenever they asked Miss Pritchard to see Muffin, she always made excuses: Muffin was sleeping, she'd just had a bath and was wet, or her stomach was upset. Tired of excuses, eventually Charlie and Patty Ann decided to take matters into their own hands. They planned to sneak into the house (even though it seemed kind of haunted) and search until they found the dog they'd heard so much about. An old house like that would surely have a window they could easily pry open.

As luck would have it, the youngsters found a small, stray Dachshund puppy wandering the train station. It was pathetic-looking and thin, as though it hadn't eaten in days. Charlie picked up the dog and they delivered it to Miss Pritchard's. She was excited to see them with the little pup.

"Oh, a wiener dog," she screeched. She explained that it was several days since she had a dog besides Muffin to care for. She readily took the stray, thanked them, and closed the door in their faces. However, while they were standing on the porch, Patty Ann took the opportunity to look intently into the room. She noticed the curtains across the room move slightly as though lifted by a slight breeze. As they walked away from the house, she told Charlie there was a possibility of an open window. Just what they needed.

A couple of hours later at about dusk, Charlie and Patty Ann returned to the creaky old house and went around back where they thought the open window might be. Sure enough, there it was! And the sill was low enough for them to crawl through with little effort. As their feet touched the floor, they heard Miss Pritchard in the kitchen talking to someone. Maybe it was Muffin, they thought.

Patty Ann and Charlie crept along the wall toward the voice. Cobwebs brushed their faces, and a musty smell filled their nostrils, but they were determined to carry out their mission even though their entire bodies shook with fear.

They peered in the slightly open kitchen door and saw Miss Pritchard sitting on the floor caring for a healthy-looking miniature poodle. The tiny dog they had brought earlier was cowering in the corner. When the poodle finished the snack placed before her and Miss Pritchard stroked her fur for the last time, she picked the dog up and walked toward the basement door. Holding the poodle in one arm, she carefully opened the door, slowly and cautiously peered in, then suddenly opened it wider, saying, "Have a nice dinner Muffin," and she threw the poodle into the basement.

Charlie and Patty Ann could barely control themselves. Shaken by what they'd seen, their first thought was to run, to get out of that house. They knew that they could not risk exposure and would have to leave as quietly as they had come, through the window, unnoticed.

Miss Pritchard, meanwhile, turned to the frightened puppy and prepared a plate for it. She gently urged, "Eat up, Sweetie, your turn is next."

While the dog was being cared for, Patty Ann and Charlie made their escape.

The next day, no one would believe what had happened. Just the wild imagination of a couple of kids, everyone thought. So the youngsters decided to prove their story was true. Armed with a digital camera, they returned to Miss Pritchard's that very night. The back window was still open, so they slipped inside.

Again, Miss Pritchard was in the kitchen tending to a lone and very scraggly dog. "This isn't much more than a snack, Muffin, but it will have to do, for now," she muttered. "We don't have time to fatten this one up to make a decent meal, so we'll go with what we've got."

Charlie prepared to get a picture of Miss Pritchard as she threw the dog into the basement, but in his anxiety to get closer, he bumped the door, which banged into a table, knocking a vase to the floor. Hearing the noise, Miss Pritchard raced from the kitchen into the room where Charlie and Patty Ann had hidden.

"Well, look here," Miss Pritchard exclaimed as she grabbed each by the arm. "It looks as if Muffin will get a full course meal after all." She dragged the kids, kicking and screaming, toward the basement door. Her fingernails dug in as they tried to pull away.

"I'm coming, Muffin, and I've got a great surprise. You'll think it's Thanksgiving."

Upon reaching the basement, Miss Pritchard tried holding both kids with one hand while opening the door. Turning the doorknob, she relaxed her grip on Charlie, who immediately flashed the camera, temporarily blinding the old lady. Patty Ann jerked loose, and as the door swung open, she pushed Miss Pritchard into the basement. The old woman stumbled, falling headfirst down the steps. Charlie slammed the door shut, and they ran to the open window.

From the basement came the frightened voice of Miss Pritchard calling, "No, Muffin, no—!" and the sound of tearing flesh and crunching bones.

A Reminder

As all around us the earth breathes in
the sun . . . Slowly, silently, we
climb down to the wide beach
and the blue waves.
In silence, we look into other's eyes . . .
and the mute stillness
of happiness will sink
upon us.

The Guardian

I see her eyes
all filled with tears
and know her heart is broken.

I long to hold her,
dismiss her fears
let her know she's not forsaken.

We'll be as one
when that time nears
our world will not be shaken.

But just for now
we will stay apart
and bear the grief we have taken.

Then as eternity rolls
and time marches on
our love will remain unbroken.

A Lunch-break Short Story

Mushrooms for Lunch

Jackie waited all semester for this date. Her heart pounded like it would come out of her chest just thinking about it. What would she wear? How would she do her hair? Where would he take her? Possibly dancing? It was just lunch, but Jackie's mind bounced from thought to thought. Sure, he was a little older (as old as her father, she would learn), and he was married. But he was so handsome, so polite, so easy to talk to. So what if he was also one of her students.

I'm tired of staying home with only Felix, the miniature poodle, for company, Jackie thought.

Living alone for twelve years with Felix in a small, crowded, but efficient apartment with dingy orange walls in every room and no storage space made Jackie somewhat bitter. After all, her divorce from a husband of only six months and the estrangement from what little family she had was reason enough to withdraw from society. She felt alone and unwanted.

But now . . .

Before she could finish the idea of her dream date, Jackie's thoughts turned negative.

What if he doesn't like me? What if I say something stupid? What if I seem too eager?

Now, wait a minute! she scolded herself. After all, I am a college professor, well-educated (finished first in my class at USC) and liked by my peers and students. Why should I be afraid?

But it has been a long time since I've dated. I wonder if he likes a lot of makeup. What should I order for lunch? Or should I let him order for me? But what if I don't like it? I'd have to eat it anyway. Ugh, stuffed portabella. I don't want to embarrass him.

I'm an adult. I know how to act. Just follow his lead, someone once told me. It will be all right. *It will be all right*—those words brought back memories from a past Jackie wanted to forget.

It will be all right, her father told her when he began abusing her at age eight.

It will be all right, when she went to school in ragged clothes and worn-out shoes because her parents spent what little money they had on booze and drugs.

It will be all right, she was told by a school counselor after being raped.

It will be all right, she told herself when she ran away from home.

It will be all right, she heard again and again—but it never was.

The one exception was when the opportunity to go to college came along. Of course, Jackie had to serve as maid, mistress, and companion to the sponsor who paid the bills.

So, being with an older man didn't really bother her. Perhaps this time it really will be all right.

Jackie gathered herself together, took a shower, laid out her best clothes, and began to apply makeup and do her hair. She had no expensive perfume, so she applied liberally from the bottle she had purchased at the drug store.

There was still an hour or more before she was to meet her date. They had decided on the park. Was that going to be the date? There were no nice places to eat near there. Surely, it wouldn't be a fast-food restaurant. But his apartment was just on the other side of the park. She knew because she followed him home one day. Was he preparing lunch for us? Or perhaps he was just getting me there, and like so many others, intended to just use me.

Fear began to creep into her mind and body. She knew it was too good to be true! He's like all the rest. It's not going to be all right. Tears welled up in her eyes. She slumped into a chair at the kitchen table and sobbed.

Jackie didn't realize how long she was in that position, but when she looked up at the clock, it was well past the meeting time. She took a plate from the cupboard, intending to make a sandwich. She put the plate on the table, and sitting in the chair, she simply stared blankly at the empty plate. Visions of a romantic lunch danced through her mind but disappeared when Felix jumped into her lap.

Just you and me, Jackie said aloud. She glanced again at the empty plate. The phone rang. She did not pick it up.

Answer to a Prayer

From the treetops tall
I heard Him speak
in answer to a prayer
that I uttered so weak.

The leaves just rustled
the trees so swayed
I fell to my knees
and again I prayed

I heard the answer
and now I know
I'll follow Him
wherever He goes.

Destiny

Though we be miles apart
you are still close by
I knew from the start
it was destiny. You and I.

What and why
I do not know
a part of life's
ebb and flow.

Though we be miles apart
you're in my mind to stay
and from mind to heart
you'll never fade away.

How and when
fate will shout
we will know
without a doubt.

Though we be miles apart
I feel your presence near
your smile has made a mark
so very, very sweet and dear.

Up and down
today, tomorrow
smile or frown
joy comes from sorrow.

Though we be miles apart
together we face the mystery
on this life we now embark
and leave the rest to history.

Listen and Hear

In the still of the night
you can hear God's words
the wind, the trees,
the crickets, the birds.

With the noise of the day
He speaks to us, too
we just need to listen
our life He'll renew.

A Shorter-Than-Most Short Story

Back Door to Compass Pointe

My son-in-law, Neil, is a golfer. He reads about it, watches it on TV, goes to the driving range, plays as often as possible, and he and my daughter plan vacations around certain golf tournaments and which courses to play. He even collects old golf balls. So, when he invited me to go on a golf-ball-collecting trip, I accepted.

I was told to wear long pants, even though it was 90 degrees, and to wear old sneakers. I would soon find out why. I dressed as directed and walked across my backyard to his. Several years ago, I gave them a neighboring lot so they could build a home. The reward for me is that my grandchildren are close by.

He took down two bicycles from the garage rafters, pumped up the tires, strapped to his bike a bag and a long-handled contraption with a ring on the end. Away we went. About five minutes later, we turned off the paved street onto a path in the woods. Neil was in front of me, and I could see him swatting at spider webs, and sometimes they would fly over his shoulder and into my face. The path narrowed the farther we rode.

Before long, dead trees and branches had to be dodged; thus, the long pants. When a log was across the path, we dismounted and carried the bikes over the obstruction. Eventually, the path became very sandy and difficult to maneuver forward. Part of the time, we walked the bikes. A long sloping hill appeared in front of us, and by the time we reached the top, I was glad I had remembered to put my nitro pills in my pocket. For a while, my chest felt like it was going to collapse.

At the top of the hill, we turned onto an even smaller and more rugged path. It was here that we ditched the bikes in the woods and went the remainder of the way on foot. Because of the dense foliage, the air was very still, and the humidity was stifling. My shirt began to show wet spots, even though I am the type that does not normally perspire much.

"Look," shouted Neil, "I've never noticed this before, and I was here just a few months ago."

It was a skull! Examination revealed it to be a deer.

Farther along the way, an old Jeep was in the ditch. Windows were broken out and a hard hat was still in the back seat. *How? Why?*

Soon, a creek crossed our path. I can jump this, I thought. I failed to take into consideration the bog on the other side; so I ended up ankle-deep in mud (thus, the old sneakers). As I looked back, there were frogs and a snake in the water—not some of my favorite things.

We soon reached the back side of the golf course. Before

long, I began to spot golf balls in the woods. I picked them up and put them in the bag Neil brought with him. He had that long-handled contraption that I soon realized was not just for knocking down spider webs but was made to pick up the balls without bending over. I should have had it—after all, I'm twenty-five years older than Neil. It was then that I realized that it was not old balls that he collected but those he could use at the driving range.

I glanced out toward the green where two golfers were teeing off. They hit the balls, got into a cart, and drove to the next tee. I wondered what they'd have thought had they seen me. They might have asked whether it was some old homeless man salvaging golf balls, thinking, My goodness, that's our pastor. What is he doing?

But I wasn't seen, and the two golfers went on their merry way, hitting balls into the woods while I picked them up for my son-in-law. He doesn't really need them; he can afford his own. He just enjoys these outings, and I'm glad I was invited on this trip. The bag was almost full in about 45 minutes, so we headed back. On the way, we stopped at a place where Neil had stashed some balls from his last trip, like a squirrel collecting hazelnuts, because he had too many balls for the bag. The bag was now full of nearly 100 balls.

We picked up our bikes and rode home a different route, passing a tract of land posted with large DO NOT

ENTER and NO TRESPASSING signs. Again, WHO? And WHY? crossed my mind.

The return trip seemed much easier, and I did not think of the Nitro pills in my pocket. When we arrived safely home, my daughter was anxiously waiting, wondering if her heart-patient father was all right. It was a good day of exploring and an opportunity to spend time with my son-in-law. I'm grateful for both.

It Hurts

It hurts, really hurts
my arms are aching
for you
my heart is breaking
for you
I try to forget
and yet
the memories are there for the taking

It hurts, really hurts
my eyes are crying
for you
my soul is dying
for you
I want your touch
so much
of my love there is no denying

It hurts, really hurts
my desire is only
for you
my being is lonely
for you
I give my life
with no strife
without you, it's forlornly

It hurts, really hurts
my joys are complete
for you
my love will repeat
for you
it's always there
and I care
I do not want defeat
BUT—it hurts, it really hurts.

Because

Can we really be this much in love?
I think so!

Can we really be this happy?
I think so!

Can we really want to be with one another all the time?
I think so!

Can we really hurt inside when we're apart?
I think so!

But how can I love you
when I hardly know you?
Because you have touched my heart!
Because in my soul I have known you forever.
And there is nothing that will keep us apart.

How can I love you
When you are miles away?
Because you have captured my very being!
In my mind you are always near
Your beautiful face I am constantly seeing.

The NASCAR Nag

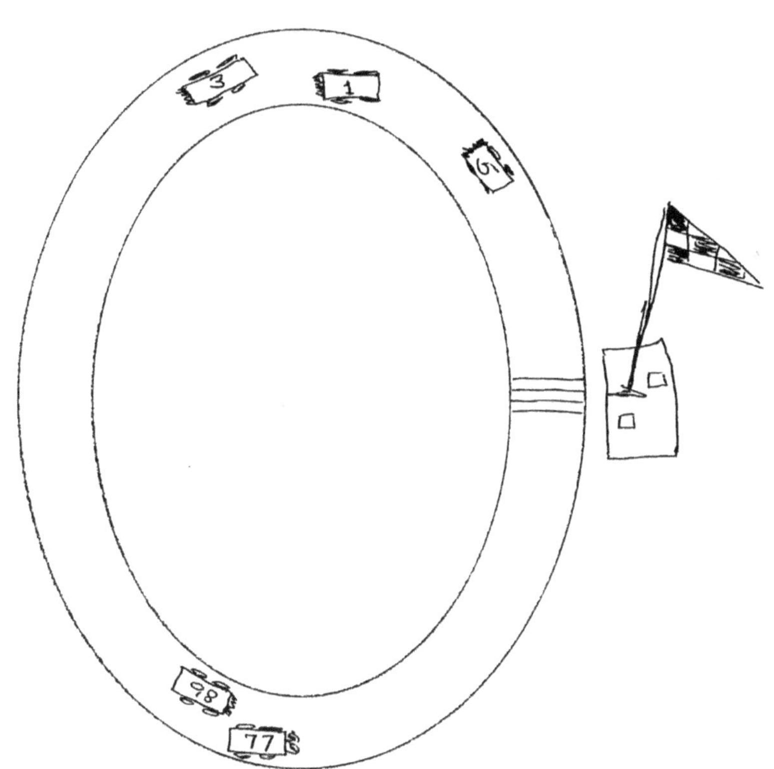

A Really Short, Short Story

The Place

The stranger approached the building hesitantly, wanting to enter but almost afraid, yet eager. This was nothing like he had ever seen or imagined. Curiosity welled within him. Questions filled his mind.

Gathering up all the courage he could muster, he walked through the doorway. A strange yet pleasant odor greeted his nostrils. The surface he walked was very hard and had a pattern throughout. Going on into the next part of the building, he noticed that the floor changed. It now was a solid color but soft to the touch. It was a huge room filled with many objects foreign to him, which also had that soft, pleasing feel.

The stranger sat cross-legged in a corner and began to take in this new environment. As his eyes gathered in all that surrounded him, his thoughts went back to just a few hours earlier. He'd been playing with his little brother on the earthen floor of a thatched hut. The playthings they found amusing were stones and odd-shaped sticks. But it was fun sitting by the light of a small, flickering fire.

This place where he now sat was different. There seemed to be openings in the wall, but they were painted over with scenes of people and places. Illuminated objects hung from the ceiling. There was no fire, yet it was warm in this building. The stranger had the feeling of not being alone, but no one else was there. At least, no one he could see.

He felt a peace come over him and was no longer afraid. Feeling safe in this new and wonderful place, he began to relax. His eyelids grew heavy, and he drifted into a deep sleep.

He jerked awake to the singing of many voices. His eyes opened to a room full of happy, jubilant people. They were singing and clapping their hands to a rhythmic beat. The stranger rose to his feet and faces smiled at him. He felt a welcoming. Before long, he was clapping and swaying to the sound of the music. That warm feeling overcame him again, and he was glad to be here in this strange place.

A Limerick

Don't want to be rude
But I like you nude
Your body thrills me
Your sweetness fills me
And I'm not being lewd.

Don't want to be haughty
But I like you gaudy
Your kisses are sweet
Your hugs are a treat
Especially when you are naughty.

Don't want to be mean
But on you I can lean
You're always there
Because you care
You make life so serene.

A Picture in a Picture

One frame
Five pictures
One Mother, five boys:

Logger
Store owner
Clergyman
Realtor
Plumber

Education
Families
Success

All in one—

A Longer-than-Most Short Story

Turn Back the Clock

Until Alex opened that door, it was a day like any other. Carrying that heavy case from house to house, saying the same pitch over and over, seeing the same dull faces (although they belonged to a million different people), and eventually, driving to another housing complex to start the same monotonous routine. The only advantage to this was that there was plenty of time to daydream and think of days gone by when life was exciting and had some meaning—days when Alex had been someone, was one of the crowd and had lots of friends.

If only he hadn't gone away and joined the service. If only he hadn't hurriedly gotten married. If only he'd gone to college. If only he'd kept in touch with her. If only. If only. But here it was lunchtime, and Alex decided to grab a quick sandwich at one of those hamburger-and-chicken places. Maybe he could make a couple of extra calls; he could use another sale this week.

As he pulled the new 1978 Ford company car into the parking slot, he noticed that three front sides of the building were glass. Inside were several people ordering or sitting at the picnic-like tables, seemingly enjoying the food. There was the usual mix of people—families, some young, others old. Hippie types, and businessmen, too. Alex sat engrossed in one of his many thoughts within the air conditioning of the car.

Almost mechanically, he got out of the car and walked to the building entry. The door opened into a poorly lit vestibule, and as Alex passed through this small, darkened area, something seemed to happen to him. Not a stark, overpowering event, but a realization that something could be amiss. It was as if he lost his balance, or Alex thought, recovering from a hangover. He shrugged it off and opened the door into the central part of the building.

It then hit him full force—this was not what he'd seen through the plate glass windows when he'd been sitting momentarily in his car out front. Where were the families? The hippies? The businessmen?

In their stead, he saw only a bunch of high-school-aged boys and girls—not the current blend of young people, but something vaguely familiar. Before he had a chance to clear his mind or set things straight, a voice interjected from the far corner of the room, "Hey Alex, here's your coffee and banana cream pie. Come get it before I eat it."

A small, thin, dark-complected girl with beautiful eyes ran up to him and put her arm in his. "What are we standing here for? I saved you a place," she cooed.

Alex was dumbfounded! This was *impossible.*

Because of the girl's slight tug on his arm, Alex stumbled a few steps forward.

"Are you all right?" she asked. Alex stopped short and stared at her. He spoke her name as a question. She said nothing, but Alex knew it was *her* and she was still seventeen years old. He started walking again toward the table in the corner where a young couple sat waiting for them. As he passed the window, he noticed his reflection in the glass. His receding hairline was gone, as were the age lines on his face. He looked past the image to the automobiles parked outside. There sat his 1946 Plymouth that he and a friend painted metallic green!

It all sank in now. He'd walked into something from twenty-five years ago. With this full realization, he held the hand that rested on his arm a little tighter. When they got to the table, Alex spoke to his pals, "Hi, you two. Been waiting long?"

"Nothing new, you're always late," said the tall, good-looking fellow moving his feet off the chair across the table.

Alex sat with a smile as he recognized his buddy and began sipping his coffee. This is too good to be true, he thought. I'm eighteen again, and everything is just as it was when I graduated high school. The same mistakes won't happen again, he reassured himself.

He glanced around the room and recognized some people immediately. A group of girls sat at a large table near the front door. Alex knew two of them. Several others were familiar, but their names did not come to mind.

"You got here just in time to leave again," the guy said. "We're going to the drive-in. Are you two coming?"

"Sure," Alex replied, glancing at the little girl beside him, getting an affirmative nod and shy smile.

"Go start the car. I'll be right out," whispered the dark-haired girl. Alex knew she must have to use the restroom, so he moved in the direction of the exit. Something made him hesitate as he started to pull open the door. Over his shoulder, Alex only got a glimpse of the one he had been dreaming about for so long as she disappeared into the rear of the building. He started to scream her name but instead opened the door and went outside.

As he stared at his aging hands, he realized there was no green Plymouth, no friends, or no eighteen-year-old self. Alex rushed back into the building he had just left. He must have had a look of horror on his face as the crowd of present-day people looked quizzically in his direction.

"Where did she go?" yelled Alex as he ran toward the back of the room. Bursting into the ladies' room, he found it empty. Before Alex could move any further, the manager grabbed him by the shoulder and insisted he leave the premises.

"I knew I shouldn't have let go of her," Alex stammered as he stumbled outside again in the awkward clutches of the manager, followed by other customers' stares. As Alex got into the car, still dazed by all that had happened, a waitress quickly passing by whispered, "Come back tomorrow at this same time." He tried stopping her, but she vanished around the building into another door. Noticing the time, it was 12:45 exactly when Alex finally drove away. He was unable to work the rest of the afternoon, thinking of all that had transpired and wondering about the next 24 hours.

That night was the most miserable of Alex's life. He couldn't sleep; he paced the floor, drank coffee, and wondered if he wasn't crazy, whether this was all another of his nutty imagination trips. But it all seemed so real! From the soft touch of her hand on his arm, talking to her, to holding her small hand, Alex thought, if I ever get to hold her again, I'll never let go. In the wee hours of the morning, he finally dozed off but woke with a start when he thought he had slept past the midday hour. It was later than usual, so he hurriedly showered, shaved, and dressed. Skipping breakfast, he drove toward the part of the city he'd been in the day before.

Alex had no desire or time to make sales calls, so he drove around until 12:15. As he pulled into the fast-food restaurant's parking lot, everything looked the same as the day before. He turned off the ignition and stared through the windshield into the distance, looking for something that might assure him it would be as he wished it would be. There was no indication of such, so he slowly moved out of the car and walked toward the front entrance. Opening the door and stepping inside, Alex noticed that same semi-nauseous sensation he had experienced the day before. This was reassuring, so he quickly walked into the main building through the vestibule.

I'm not crazy, Alex thought as he heard a Johnnie Ray tune playing on the jukebox and saw some old friends crowded around the soda fountain.

"What happened to you last night?" a voice from the back of the room asked.

Alex turned, and there she was. For a moment, he was unable to speak. His heart pounded as if it would burst from his chest. "I'm sorry about that, but please don't ask. Can you possibly forgive me?" Alex finally was able to say. He reached out, and she slipped her soft, small hands into his. She seemed to understand what Alex was going through.

"Can we go for a ride?" she asked.

He hesitated for a moment, thinking about what might happen.

"Only if you hold onto me tight all the way," Alex finally answered affectionately.

The tiny girl with dark skin and big eyes looked at him and answered with a voice that let Alex know everything was going to be all right. "You know I'll never let go," she said.

Alex thought of his vow the night before and clasped her hands even more tightly.

Hand in hand, they started toward the exit. Before Alex could push open the door, the waitress who told him to return stood in his way. "Go out the back door, please," she stated firmly.

They turned and walked past all the tables and out the rear exit. As soon as they were outside, Alex looked at his companion for a moment and then they held each other closely without a word.

They scampered out of the alley into the street at the front of the building. There it was—the green Plymouth. Euphoria filled Alex's very being. It *was* real. As they drove away, Alex thought, somehow, we were able to turn back the clock.

Nonsense

With apologies to

Ogden Nash

And

Dr. Seuss

I submit the following:

120

Question:

How far is it from somewhere to nowhere?

121

Answer:

Maybe a day – maybe twenty-four hours, depending on the route taken and whether you are coming or going!

Could I? Would I?

Could I love you more?
Even if I could
Would I love you more?
Could I want you more?
Even if I did
Would I want you more?
Could I?
Would I?
I do.

Poo

We went on vacation
and I had to poo—
I said to my sweetheart
go find something else
to do
so she went
and I did, too!

A Postscript to
The Twelve Days of Christmas

The pear tree died
And the partridge flew away.
The swans went upstream
And the pipers didn't play.
The maids refused to work
And the Ladies didn't dance.
The doves were not in love
And the Lords didn't prance.
The drummers lost their sticks
And the birds didn't call.
The hens went back to France
And the geese laid not at all.
That leaves only one.
And to you, this I bring
My eternal love
And five gold rings.

If

If trees could sneeze
They'd bend way down
And wipe their noses
Upon the ground.

If grass could talk
Like most of us
When walked upon
They'd probably cuss.

If weeds could bleed
Like people do
There'd be no green
Just a reddish hue.

If rocks could fly
Like south-bound geese
They'd leave this place
For profound peace.

Angel

I call her
Angel face
There is no one
To take her place.

I see her
Angel eyes
When I'm with her
How time flies.

I touch her
Angel skin
I melt like ice
From deep within.
I hear her
Angel voice
That lovely sound
Makes me rejoice.

I taste her
Angel lips
My heart stands still
While doing flips.

I smell her
Angel glow
How I love her
She must know.

The Retort of Beverly Blankenship

She was just a young girl

Innocent

And plain

Some called her ugly

The old man teased her incessantly

Threatening to kiss her

Playfully

But she was embarrassed

Or so it seemed

The old man was stopped in his tracks

When one day

She responded

With a crowd looking on

"Do it and talk about it later!"

Good or Bad

Liver—makes me quiver
While
Jello—makes me mellow

Who

He didn't miss his passes
Even though his name was Plunkett
He was right on target
Who woulda thunk it?

We call it a houseboat
They say it's a junket
But they're both made for living
Who woulda' thunk it?

He's seven feet tall
And surely can dunk it
There's a girl that can do it
Who woulda thunk it?

They said it was unsinkable
What was it that had sunk it?
Just a piece of ice
Who woulda thunk it?

I don't want to be alone
Even when I "Monk" it
But we're together now
Who woulda thunk it?

Pets

A dog
A cat
A pony
Too many pets
Is a lot of baloney

Turtles and Butterflies

Turtles and Butterflies
What a pair!
One travels on the ground
The other in the air!

One is slow
And sticks his head out
The other has wings
And flies all about.

One is hard
The other soft
One is grounded
The other aloft

Which would you be?
What's your choice?
They can't answer
For neither has voice.

Metatarsal

The word metatarsal
Is not universal
Certainly not haughty
Nor is it naughty

You're almost alone
If you know it's a bone
But no one knows
It's part of your toes.

I Wish

I wish—I wish—Oh, how I wish
That I could get my wishes

Then every night after supper
Someone else would do the dishes.

Positive Thinking

I sat and thought
What I ought
And accomplished absolutely nothing.

But then I thought
What I ought not
And I got something.

This goes to show
Ain't what you know
But how you go about it.

With no reserve
I got what I deserve
And you better not doubt it.

Me—Oh My!

My hair is thin
I'm getting bald
But on my chin
I have it all

My teeth are false
But they don't ache
A bit of apple
I cannot take

My eyes are weak
I hardly see
I need my specs
Most definitely

My poor feet hurt
Most all the time
Before I die
I'll end this rhyme

The Garden

Dig the ground
Plant the seed

Water the sprout
Pull the weed

Spray the bug
Till the row

Fence the plot
Scare the crow

Pick the crop
Eat the best

Enjoy the taste
Freeze the rest

Like the food
Hate the work

Plan the next
Who's the jerk?

Friends

What are friends made of?
Good friends are made of nothing
No grief—no sorrow
No lend—no borrow
No joy—no tears
No talk—no fears
What are friends made of?
Maybe love.

Hot Dog

Mustard and ketchup on a bun
Makes a hotdog lots more fun

The NASCAR Nag

"I told you Blue and White"

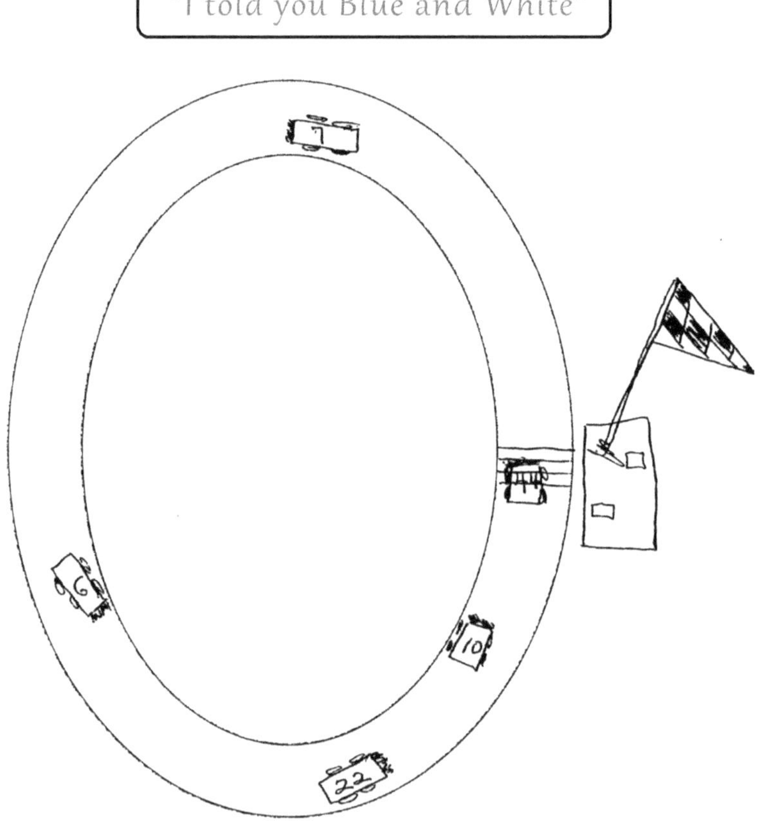

An Adventure Short Story

Waterloo

It was eighty-seven degrees on that summer day when Joan and Jerry decided to go to the old swimming hole. They both turned sixteen that year and were well on their way to adulthood.

"Don't go near the falls. It's dangerous," they'd been told.

"We're not children, Mom," Joan retorted. So off they went.

It was just a short walk to the river and then a stroll to the pool, where the water ran still and deep. But ninety yards downstream, the banks of the river closed in and forced the stream to become a raging torrent. This was "the falls." Many had fallen in and been swept away. And so it was that the children were told to "not go near the falls."

The temptation was too strong. They couldn't stay away. The thrill of the force of the water was euphoric. And besides that, they might happen upon the treasure "hidden in the cleft of the rock," or so the legend goes.

Curiosity and thrill-seeking took over. Maybe there was treasure. If not, what fun it would be!

Jerry announced after an hour or so, "One more dive before we go. It's getting late."

They jumped in together hand in hand and were swept a longer than usual distance when they came up for air. Looking toward the shore, neither recognized the beach, the tree line, or anything else.

"Where are we?" Joan asked. No answer came from Jerry, who was trying to go ashore.

Save myself, then save Joan. That's what he was taught. Even though young and healthy, athletic, and strong, as well as an excellent swimmer, he made no headway against the force of the water. He turned his attention to Joan. She was also an exceptional swimmer, so together, they fought toward the stream bank.

Making little progress, the two decided to go with the current and see where it would take them. Maybe to a spot where the force of the water was not so strong. But suddenly, a giant hole opened up in the water, whirling in a counterclockwise direction.

The whirlpool sucked them in deeper and deeper, but there was no trouble breathing as if there was no water at all. The deeper the pair went, the murkier the water became. They could not speak, and it was then that Jerry noticed Joan was naked. The force of the whirling water had simply ripped off her bikini. Jerry took off his swimming trunks and gave them to her to avoid further embarrassment.

The deeper they went, the more cognizant they were of

their surroundings as the water cleared. A large school of fish appeared in the distance. It seemed as if they all were looking at Joan and Jerry as they passed by in a whirl.

"Don't tell, don't tell," they all said in unison.

A large octopus came out of their midst, tentacles searching for something or someone more significant than the tiny silver fish surrounding Joan and Jerry. Suddenly, the fish were gone, but their words echoed throughout, "Don't tell."

Hundreds of crabs, turtles, and frogs swam toward the kids from the left and right. A seahorse was leading them. "Don't tell, don't tell," they were heard to say. The seahorse spoke, "Follow me!"

As the swarms of various water denizens gathered behind him, Joan and Jerry joined them. They were led to a graveyard of sunken battleships, a schooner, a dingy, many canoes, sailboats, a paddleboat, and many other large and small watercraft.

Joan and Jerry were at the center of critters and boats, astounded by their wonder. "Don't tell, don't tell," resounded through the wonder of it all.

Surrounding the fantastic scene was the most astonishing coral, turning from green and gold to orange and purple, to magenta and yellow, while shimmering silver throughout. Even flashes of blue and red could be seen.

Guarding all this was an enormous pterodactyl, nearly

ninety feet in length and weighing in excess of four thousand pounds. The creature flew around and around the underwater graveyard looking for intruders. Joan and Jerry were the exceptions—they were escorted into this amazing place. In a moment of reflection, Jerry wondered how all this could be within that little creek they'd jumped into only moments ago. Suddenly, an alligator-like creature swam near them with a mouthful of something. He dropped it at their feet. Picking it up, Joan discovered it was a bikini top fashioned of seaweed. Donning the apparel, they continued forward.

In the distance, a dark cloud was rapidly approaching, and when it reached them, they were caught up in an underwater geyser, an under-the-surface waterspout. In a matter of seconds, they were thrust to the surface. The first thing they saw was the Waterloo Bridge, where they'd started.

"We haven't moved at all," exclaimed Jerry. "What was all that about?"

Everyone on shore was hissing, pointing fingers, and booing. Joan and Jerry had hardly moved from where they jumped in. It seemed as if the rapids were not even there.

"What have you guys been doing under there?" someone shouted.

As they climbed out of the water, Joan checked the

bikini. It was intact—no seaweed—and Jerry had trunks again. "We'll talk later," Jerry whispered, "and try to figure this out."

That evening, during their muted conversation, two butterflies, one yellow and one white, appeared and began to tell the secret.

The butterflies spoke in hushed tones. "You saw only a small portion of what is down there. In its entirety, the coral is the essence of life and must be protected at all costs and for all time. Periodically, a small fragment of the coral will come loose and float upward. When it reaches the surface, it becomes earth-like. Perhaps a tree, a mountain, a pet, a person, even a butterfly. Thus, we are here."

The pair listened intently.

"You," they continued, "were chosen to know the secret because of the kind hearts that beat within each of you and with the assurance that the secret will be safe with you. An earthly representative is needed because of the condition of humanity. Should that deteriorate even more, the coral must be warned. That is where you and your descendants come in. Keep the secret—warn the coral. You now know the way to get there and will be protected at all times."

As the butterflies concluded, they said, "That's the treasure of legend—Life itself. Begin by guarding against the destruction of the rapids and the falls. Let no one know what is below the surface of the stream. Speak not of this conversation." With that final admonition, the butterflies disappeared into the night.

Joan and Jerry simply looked at one another without a word being spoken. They said good night and went to their own homes.

Several years later, Jerry and Joan were married. Neither of them had spoken about their fantastic adventure nor their responsibility to guard the coral. But within their hearts, they wondered.

Unknown to them, the butterflies had also spoken to their children and grandchildren when they reached age sixteen, just as they had spoken with Jerry and Joan. As instructed, these offspring told no one, nor had they discussed it among themselves.

The secret was kept—the treasure was found. Joan and Jerry, children and grandchildren, had each been taken on that same underwater adventure without the others being aware that they knew.

Secret told—Secret revealed.

Treasure found—Treasure kept.

An Endless Short Story

The House

The house on Pomegranate Way was a beautiful, subtle tan color during the day. But once dusk came upon the land, it took on a darker, more sinister shade of brown, with streaks of mahogany and brindle that seemed to move with the wind. And then, when the early morning sun shone through the trees and dew was on the tall fescue grass surrounding the front and back yards, the house responded to the sun's warmth with anger. Shutters banged, doors slammed, and even the roof attempted to keep away the morning rays.

It could not. By mid-morning, the beauty of the old structure was evidence of its once glorious past. Why all the fury at daybreak? What had happened?

No one had lived there for many years. Decades ago, the house rang with laughter and frivolity. Children played on the well-kept lawns now overrun with weeds and thistle. Music could be heard from as far away as the small Methodist church up the road. The house was happy and full of love and joy.

Abandoned, the house was now filled with animosity, resentment, and feelings of revenge. The house had reason to feel that way. After all, it wasn't the house's fault. It had tried, hanging onto the peeling paint as long as it could. It hurt when the floors buckled. It cried as the windows clouded with grime so they couldn't be seen through. But what could the house do? It couldn't repave the driveway leading to the place. It couldn't reshingle the roof when neglect allowed wind and rain to penetrate. Cold winter nights froze water pipes and hot, muggy summer days began to rot the foundation.

No wonder the house was angry. "Fixer-Upper." The house had never heard such a phrase before, but when the young couple came to visit, that was the expression they used when referring to all the house's problems. What did "fixer-upper" involve? What did that even mean?

Going into the attic? Hope not. What was there and what happened there must remain a secret. Even if it meant the end. The end of the house in its glory had already happened; would this mean the end entirely? No more worrying about the elements. Just let it all go?

No! The house could not let that happen.
The couple took a cursory look and decided they wanted to do a more thorough inspection. They would be back in two weeks.

Despite its history and feelings held, the house finally realized it could not just stand by and allow the possibility of the attic's exposure to happen. Though the house was angry and upset about the last several years of abandonment, it could not let it fall into nothingness.

The door to the attic had not been opened for years. As a matter of fact, it had been nailed shut. The house waited until midnight to gain access when a storm was expected. At its peak, the house shook loose the moorings that held the door tightly closed. Visitors would simply think that lightning strikes knocked them loose. But the house knew better.

The open door created a vacuum so strong that even some furniture was moved. A large pile of discarded clothes, bedding, and stuffed animals had been piled in the darkest corner of the room to hide a small opening. It seemed that the secret was about to be exposed.

The house was frightened. Maybe the secret will be kept after all. The door opened into a long, dark hallway that led to a much larger room. In that larger room was a stairway with a door at the top. Behind the door was a solid brick wall with a beautiful pattern of reddish and purple streaks. In preparation for the visitors' return, the house girded all its strength to keep the wall intact. The dampness of the room added to the moisture on the stairway.

The house smiled in appreciation. Maybe this would hasten the couple's retreat from the attic if they thought there was nothing there, just a wall. When the young couple returned, they were brought up to date on the recent storm and the damage it caused. They went to see for themselves. But the house was prepared. Let them see the room that the wind put into disarray. Satisfy their curiosity. Just a peek, but not beyond. Not seeing behind the brick wall would take care of their need and maintain the integrity of what was there.

Maybe it would be a good thing after all. As long as the wall stood firm. The house seemed happy.

Would it be restored to its former glory? The house hoped so. But the wall….

The couple returned. The woman fell in love with the house immediately. The man was dubious. As his wife looked inside, he inspected the outside. Something was just not right. There seemed to be more to the outside of the house than the interior room layout suggested. The walls did not match. He went inside to that part of the house where he noticed the alignment disparity from the outside. That led him to the attic.

The house had rearranged the room so that the opening for that tiny door could not be found easily. The wall took a deep breath and waited.

The attic, the small opening, the stairway, the door, the brick wall, intrigued the man and made him desire the house even more so. The agreement on the purchase of the house was completed. The house was happy. The couple would restore the glorious old days when the house held some stature in the neighborhood.

But as they were leaving, the house heard them talking about what they would do to the place: remove that smelly old fireplace; replace the lighting with new, modern fixtures; tear out those creaky floors and install carpeting; and, finally, knock down that stupid brick wall in the attic to discover what was behind it.

No, no! the house screamed. That wasn't the plan. We can't let that happen. The wall agreed with the house.

Three days later, the man returned with a sledgehammer, a jackhammer, picks and shovels, and many other tools for demolition. He had plans for readying the house for a make-over. He would work well into the night, catch a few hours of sleep, and begin again in the morning. His wife would come later in the day after finishing her work as a design engineer. She had prepared the plans for the make-over and was quite happy with the results, much to the chagrin of the house. She was as culpable as her spouse.

When she arrived, he was not to be found anywhere. Finally, she went to the attic, found the small opening, squeezed through, went upstairs, and opened the door. Her husband's headless body greeted her, crumpled onto the floor with multiple wounds covering him. One brick from the top of the wall, apparently loosened, fell, and struck him. The brick lay beside him, covered in blood and hair.

Still, there was no accounting for all his other wounds.

All his tools were arranged neatly in the corner of the room, except for the jackhammer. It was missing!

The young woman heard noise from behind the wall, like shutters banging, but not really that kind of noise. It was more like—a jackhammer. Suddenly, blood began to ooze out from between the bricks. As the red liquid ran down the wall, it enhanced the decorative pattern already there.

This caused the wall to sigh in relief.

Overcome with hysteria, the woman ran screaming from the room, tripping and falling as she went. Until she reached the front door. Still stunned by fear, she stumbled out the door and down the path, away from the house. In her hurry, she tripped on the narrow cobblestone sidewalk next to a deep ravine and fell headlong to her death.

The front door winked, thinking that maybe next time, older, more mature buyers would keep the Italianate style, which was what the house desired.

The wall smiled; actually, it was more of a smirk, knowing that older buyers would not find their way to it.

The secret was safe for now.

The house approved.

KID STUFF

By

Stacy

W. Henry

Joshua

David

The Sky

By Stacy, age 10

Why is the sky up so high?
Do you know why?
Neither do I.

Does the sky lie or does it fly?
Is that how it got up there so high?
Do you know why? Neither do I?

Is the sky blue or is it green?
I never seen
The sky green.

Maybe the sky's red. Does it sleep in bed?
Is the sky gold? That's what I've been told.

Now it is night. I say good night.
Good night sky.

Rock Your Way to Heaven

By Stacy, age 12

Rock away, away to heaven
Way beyond the hills

I should of listened to the
Doctor and not have taken those
Pills.

The Stars and dots and lots of colors

I knew I just did wrong.
Listen to the radio, it was now playing
My song.

A song of Rock…
A Rock-n-Roll song
I remember it well till I said
So long.

I rocked my way to heaven way
Beyond the hills
I rocked my way to heaven
All because of those pills.

The Orthodontist

By Stacy, age 12

Food all stuck in sister's braces
I don't think is very gracious.

Benji

By Stacy, age 12

Benji baby, I love you so.
But now you know you got to go.
Benji darling, say good bye.
I love you Benji, you're going to die.
Now I pray beside me bed.
To my Benji. Now he's dead.

First best poem of Lake Shore
Elementary

Read aloud to the school by

John Maranto

My School

Written by Stacy Alberts, age 12

My school ain't cool
But then, it's neat
The girls ain't groovy
But very boutique

The boys are shy
But never cry
They yell, they scream, and always gleam
At the girls, that is
Especially Liz

I like my school so very much
I like the teachers telling me to hush
I like my school, I really do
If you come here, you will too.

Come to my school
And then you can see
My school ain't the best
But good enough for me

The Flowers

By Stacy, age 12

The flowers grow with all
Their might.

I think they're such a
Pretty sight.

They grow in front of
Our back yard

They try to grow
And try real hard.

Although they're tiny,
And so very small.

I really like them,
I like them all!

Easter Bunny

By Stacy, age 12

Easter bunny come alive
I don't think you're any jive.
I know your eyes and ears are red,
You fill our baskets while we're in bed.

Easter bunny tell me true
Are you pink or are you blue?
Is your mom gray or tan?
Tell me, tell me, if you can.

Easter bunny if you know
I love you, honest, I love you so.
Easter's coming so hurry soon
And please, bunny, bring me a balloon.

Winds

By Stacy, age 12

The whistle of the winds
You can hear them far away.

But today the rain
Has taken over, the
Winds have gone astray.

The Swing Set

By Stacy, age 12

The swing set with it's
Bright red shiny color
Glitters from a distance
If you look at it from the bottom of the hill
It looks like the swing set
Is standing still.

But I know a secret
I'll never tell, I know
The secret very well.

Douglas A. Alberts

The Cricket

By Stacy, age 12

The cricket's voice awakened me
Throughout the town, above the sea.
Day to day I hear him call,
Mr. Cricket loves us all.

The Match

By Stacy, age 13

Lantern lightens by the flick
Of a match.
A match I've never seen,
A match that is not ordinary red
But a match that is half green.

The green match with it's fire burning
I didn't want it out
Momma warned if it burned too
Fast throw it down the spout.

But I watched, the match burn
Slowly, I knew it was almost done
But I would not listen
Listen to anyone.

I wish I did not light that match
now that I'm here alone
Laying in the cemetery
All I do is moan.

I Apologize

By Stacy, age 13

I'm sorry to hear about your accident
Especially when
I found out
You were born that way
I apologize.

I'm sorry I pushed your son
Into the lake yesterday but he had
To pee and it wasn't raining
I apologize

I'm sorry your back yard is missing but we
Lived in the city and didn't
Have one
I apologize.

I'm sorry I turned on the lights
Last night when you had company
But the flashlight didn't work

I apologize.
I'm sorry your grandmother
Is senile, but I needed
To practice on the bugle
I apologize.

I'm sorry your tires are flat
But I needed some fresh air
I apologize.

Douglas A. Alberts

Roll, Roll, Roll Away

By Stacy, age 13

I've rolled over here,
I've rolled over there,
Now if you don't mind
I'll roll under the chair.

Chicken

By Stacy, age 13

Chicken with your yellow beak
Always running to find or seek
Your lashes flutter on and off
Peeping perfect without a cough

Up in the air there is your tail
Perfect fur without a scale.

Tiny feet all even webbed
Tiniest I've seen
Perfect little chicken
Never even mean.

Cuddle

By Stacy, age 13

Cuddle me within your arms
Hold me tighter than ever
I need your love, so don't
Let me go. No, not never.
Let's fly away holding each
Other tight. No time to argue,
No time to fight.
Bring no money, bring no
Food. Just bring yourself
All for me.
To cuddle me, to cherish
And most of all to love.
That's all we need to fly
Up above.

Thanksgiving Day

By Stacy, age 13

Under the long grass
Little roads run
Carefully hidden
From the sun.

The blind grey mole
And slimy snake
Lie safely in the homes
That they make.

Though underneath,
Quite hidden away
Small creatures keep
Thanksgiving Day.

The Sunshine

By Stacy, age 13

Sunshine with your yellow color
Bright as you can be

Highest up in the sky
Taller than any tree

Sunshine lightens all the world
But then at night it falls

It waits for midnight soon to come
It listens for its calls

Soon its night, the sky turns dark
Dark as it could be

Sunshine soon appears again
Taller than any tree.

Doggie

By Stacy, age 14

The doggie in the window
He looks so very sad
Nobody wants to buy him
Everyone thinks he's bad.
But the doggie in the window
Only I know him well.
He really is a good doggie
But only I can tell.
So I bought the doggie
And I named him Mel
Now me and doggie get along real well.

Decision

By Stacy, age 13

When I was young
I'd sit and I'd think
Writing it down on paper with ink.
A job is what
I had to find
If only I could make up my mind.

At four or five
I wanted to be
A lighthouse keeper watching the sea.
At six I concluded
To do my own thing
I'd be a singer although I can't sing.
For a long time then
Seven to ten
I wanted to be opposite and work with the men.

A policeman is what
I decided to be
But no one on the force wanted to take me.
So ten until now
I sit and I think
Writing it down on paper with ink.

Love at First Hamburger

By Stacy, age 14

It was late, I broke my date
Had to get away
I rushed around from sky to ground,
Looking for a hamburger.

Then at the corner of Maple Street
Lighted up in the sky
Big and juicy as it seemed to be
I had to give it a try.

The joint was packed but I didn't care
I needed something to eat.
Then the waitress came to me saying: here,
Would you like a seat?

With a glass of cold water in her hand
And her posture that I could not stand
She asked what I'd like to eat.
I replied: a patty of meat.

Patiently waiting with my stomach giving a growl
I saw *my* hamburger coming towards me
And thought in my head:
Oh Wow!

She placed it right in front of me
Tall as it seemed to stand
What a great hamburger
It was bigger than I had planned.

Getting ready to take a bite, with ketchup dribbling
down
Lettuce and tomato
Piled up tall,
Wondering if I could eat it all.

I knew I could not do it
I had to keep it safe;
Away in a certain spot
But to eat it, I could not

Now and then I check on it and make sure it's okay
Although it's lettuce is shriveled
I love it every day.

Night/Morning

By Stacy, age 15

Night.
Cold airy winds.
Trees swaying.
Wind howling.
Windows clamping.
Still.
Birds.
Daybreak.
Sunshine.
Morning.

The Lake

By Stacy

In the night, very black.
Two people like to snack.
The lake reflects a full moon,
They swim perfectly in tune.
Their hearts beat very fast,
I found you at last.

The next morning she looks at him,
Then turns the lights very dim.
He asks: do you…?
She says: I do.
I will always,
Love you.

Last Night I Dreamed

By Stacy, age 15

Last night I dreamed
Of yes … another
I called him friend
I called him lover

He showed me passion
He took me in
Yet in a dream
I could not sin.

When I was down
My soul discouraged
He gave me gifts …
All kinds he flourished.

We meet in secret
Romance in the air
Rushing back to reality
With no time to spare.

It was there the dream ended.
As I lay awake
I realized
I had made a horrendous mistake.

My lightbulb
Above me
Went off
And I knew
My dream of *another*
All along – it was you.

Wildlife

By Stacy

The flowers, the trees, and the birds
That sing – softly you can
Hear.
Soon they will disappear.

Man kills its wildlife for
The sport of it.
God be with the birds, trees,
The grass, our forest.
The chipmunks chatter and play
In the sun while the squirrels gather nuts
For the winter season.

The grass on the ground soon turns
To snowy ice and the weeds are
Hidden from the playful mice.
The forest and wildlife is the best thing
In the world in any season
I hope its still there when
I get older.

My Daddy

By Stacy, age 22

My Daddy knows Jesus
He speaks of his will
Thou shalt not steal
Thou shalt not kill

My Daddy knows Jesus
He's good and he's pure
My Daddy knows Jesus
My Dad I adore.

My Daddy knows Jesus
Together they walk
Sometimes when I'm watching
Together they talk

My Daddy knows Jesus
And I know him too
Why – he introduced us!
I'll introduce you

Motocross
(The Race)

By Joshua A. Metzler, age 18

Motocross is very exciting,
If you're in the stands,
Or on the bike.

When you smell the gasoline,
And hear the engines revving,
Then your name announced over the mike.

You can tell the race will start soon,
There's nothing like the thrill,
Of 30 at the gate.

Trying to get the hole shot
Is the hardest part,
There's no time for you to wait.
Every lap counts, even if you're in first
Because one wrong move and,
You could lose it and fall.

You need to know your bike,
And what it can handle,
To ride better than them all.

Crossing the finish line,
Hearing the fans,
It's your turn to win.

Standing at the winner's circle,
With trophy and ribbon in hand,
Nothing on your face but dirt and a grin.

The Germ

By W. Henry, age 15

In my heart there swims a germ,
He cleans my heart like the worm.
The worm is tough,
He chews and chews.
Like the dove
They never lose.
I wish the worm to go and play,
But do come back another day.
I love them both, please do not fight.
Why don't you stay and spend the night?

The Worm

By W. Henry, age 15

On the ground there walks a dove,
He eats the worms of happiness.
In my heart I love the dove,
He eats the worms but makes the mess.
In my heart I love the worm,
He eats the dirt and cleans the ground.
In my heart I love the sea,
Swallowing the bird and me.
I now live deep within,
I wish the sea, did not grin.
Now the worm can clean the ground
Where I was lost and never found.

Gran'pa

By Your Grandson, David Heath III, age 12

I'm glad I have a gran'pa
Like you
Who cares about the things
I do.
He gives me coins, he gives
Me pins.
He's my favorite, he always
Wins.
He loves us both with all
His heart.
He always tries to do
His part.
Thanks for always being
There,
I know you love me and
You care.

I Prayed for You

By Your Grandson, with Love, David

I prayed for you when you felt bad,
When you were in the hospital,
I was sad.
I hope you feel better,
I want you to know,
Don't leave me,
I don't want you to go.
I wrote this poem thinking of you,
Thank you for the things you do.
I know that you will always be
A gran'pa who is always
There for me.

A Final, Not-So-Short, Short Story

Reunion: A Love Story

Based on True Happenings

The old man sat on the porch of the little cabin in the woods where the river meets the ocean. At his feet was a small child.

"Grandpa," the little boy asked, "how old are you and Grandma?"

"We're both well over one hundred, my boy," the old man answered.

"And how long have you been married?" queried the youngster. "A long time I guess, huh?"

"Why no," came the reply, "just a few short years."

The boy looked puzzled. "What about all those other years?"

"Well, that's a long, long story . . ." He paused. "But before I begin with that story let me tell you some history. You know Granny went to Heaven a long time ago."

The boy nodded affirmation.

"And Grandpa was alone for a long, long time."

Another nod.

"So when another lady came into Grandpa's life, you and all the other children called her Grandma." He looked at the boy squinting up at him. "Understand?" A third nod that the boy did.

Then began a . . . *Grandpa always said* … followed by some kind of cliché, a *when I was a kid tale*, a *parable*, or *an analogy, a warning, advice,* and sometimes even *sage words of wisdom.*

But the little boy knew this was different. The twinkle in Grandpa's eyes told him so. So, he listened intently.

"Those early years began in the Summer of 1947," Grandpa began, "and my family headed to California! We had no job, no place to live, and did not know anyone, but we were on our way. I was only twelve, the middle child of five boys ages 7 to 15 years old, when we left the comfort of a little country farm in central Oregon." He took a breath. "I was told it was because of my stepfather's health. He was about fifteen years Mom's senior. It was assumed that the warmer and drier California climate would cure the problem."

"Temporary lodging was a huge tent pitched in a city park. Then the tent was moved to an almond orchard; while we awaited the cleaning of an abandoned chicken house. It was then that a run-down former German

Prisoner of War (POW) camp was converted to barely livable homes and apartments. This is where we settled and where I spent my teen years.

"My brothers and I had many adventures living at *the camp*. On one occasion, I cut through the back path from the camp to a girl's home about three blocks away. I went under the pretext of hanging out with her brother, but I wanted to see her. I knew she would not give me a second look (she was a senior in high school and I was only a freshman) but to this very day, she was, to me, the most beautiful girl in school.

"As I approached the tiny creek between the wire enclosure of the camp (wire remaining from POW days), a shadow of a figure leaped out from the darkness toward me. Startled, afraid, yet determined, I ran in the direction of the creek and the fence, knowing there was an opening big enough for my escape from, I was certain, the ghost of an imprisoned Nazi, ready to avenge the incarceration of himself and others.

"Making it safely through the hole in the fence and over the tiny waterway, I vowed never to repeat this story, fearing the ridicule of my peers, and the fact that I'd wet my pants. And, after all that, the senior girl was not home. But I chased the dream.

"My boy, be sure to always chase your dream, wherever it takes you!"

"So, time passed. I thought I'd found another girl, but this one had a little sister.

"A cute little, blonde, curly-haired girl knew that her big sister's new boyfriend (that was me) was coming to visit, so she planned to make things as miserable as she could for them.

"Boys, phooey! she must have thought. Who needs them? So, she plotted. I won't let them be alone, I'll be everywhere they are … and she was.

"That was our informal introduction, not knowing it would be many years before we would meet again."

The little boy at his feet immediately saw the glint in Grandpa's eyes grow brighter and more intense as he thought about that first meeting with the little curly-haired girl so many years ago.

He recalled what was said. "Get away—you're annoying us. Leave us alone! was all that we could think of to say to the persistent little scamp. All to no avail. That was the last attempt made for a date with the big sister. The little sister prevailed. Did she know something that we did not?

"Years went by. I left home, went into the service, had a life. Then things changed.

"I didn't expect much of a high school reunion. After all, it had been seventy years. Most of my class of twenty-one students were either dead or could not be found. Some just flat-out refused to participate."

The little boy interrupted. "Did you have to walk ten miles in your bare feet when you were in school?"

"No, just two miles—and we did have shoes. It was a one-room schoolhouse with all eight grades attending. The total student body was less than 25 most years. It was when we got to California that I attended a larger school. It was still very small by today's standards, but much larger than that little school way out in the country where I was the only one in the 5th grade.

"Hand-me-downs, huh! Let me tell you about hand-me-downs," Grandpa went on. "By the time clothes went through two other brothers and then me, there wasn't much left of them, so new ones were bought – to fit the fourth brother, while we all had worn-out to nearly unwearable. Ahh – such is the life of a third child.

"But, back to my story. During the intervening years, there was military service. I served as a non-commissioned intelligence officer in the Far East Air Command headquartered near Tokyo, Japan. I was a cryptologist, breaking coded messages to determine flight routes of all aircraft near the Sea of Japan, and even some distance inland in order to find airfields and military installations. Like Gary Powers and U2s, remember? Naw, you're too young.

"On one occasion, I was to accompany such a flight because I'd memorized the key to the codes and did not have to take printed material. This precaution was in case we were shot down and it was discovered that we knew that particular code. No communication would be necessary between the plane and headquarters. By the way, the plane had no fire power – if we were detected, we just had the ability to get away as fast as possible, unless we encountered MiGs.

"At the conclusion of the recon flight, we turned for home – Shiroi AFB. Suddenly, I noticed a blip on the radio. I put on the headphones and set about interpreting the incoming coded messages that we'd intercepted. I discovered that three MiG-15s were on our tail. Knowing that we could not outrun them, we flew as low as possible, practically skimming the tiny waves on the Sea of Japan. The MiGs could not follow, nor could they detect us at that low altitude, and we returned to base safely.

"After military service, there was college. I already had accumulated several credit hours through the college level GED exam that I took while deployed. Then classes at Sacramento Junior College, and at Johns Hopkins University while stationed at Ft. Meade, MD, after returning stateside.

"My studies slowed somewhat while I was getting married, raising a family that includes you (the boy smiled) by myself. I was also serving as a part-time Pastor at a nearby church. But with determination and grit, after 12 long years I was awarded a Master of Divinity Degree from the Southern Baptist Theological Seminary in Louisville, KY.

"That is what's called staying power, my boy. For the next 40 years, I served pastorates in the Baltimore and Washington, DC, area."

Grandpa went on. "A few years later I considered my high school reunion – the one I was telling you about when we started, remember? I said I hadn't expected much.

"Well, surprise, surprise! I sat across the room from a woman I thought was quite attractive. I inquired who she was and was told she was a classmate's younger sister. This woman was the *little sister* who persistently bugged her elder sister and me when we were trying to have a date so many years before! Boy, had she grown up. I introduced myself, we had a short conversation, the reunion ended, and I went home – three thousand miles away.

"The next year, she was there again. We had a longer conversation. But again, the celebration ended and I went home."

The boy thought, there was that look again, the sparkle in Grandpa's eyes. "That's what keeps me going," he would say. And then continue with – "She's one in a million, and just as pretty today as she was seventy years ago – and just as lively," as he chuckled.

"But back to my story. Two months after the reunion, I

was given her phone number and was told I could call if I wanted to. I did, and we have been together since that day.

"Remember what Grandpa said: You're never too old for romance. Love is everlasting. True love will find you out.

"In a way, Grandma and I have always been together—we just didn't know it. It took us nearly seventy years to find each other again, but it was worth the wait."

The little boy got up from his sitting position, approached the old man, kissed him on the cheek, and thanked him for the story. He turned and left.

The old man felt a warmth in his heart, knowing the boy would grow up with a better understanding of what kindness, patience, and love was all about.

Three Kinds of Love

As the little boy turned down the lane to his house, he thought: Grandpa says, if you wait long enough, time will pass. And good things come and go, but mediocre hangs around all the time. And do your best and your best will do you.

Sometimes, he thought, Grandpa starts with: *when I was a kid*, and ends with a lesson that we need to learn, like putting the cart before the horse, whatever that means.

Some of those words were hard to figure out; but in the end, we knew we were told something that would make us better people.

One of Grandpa's favorites is: *If it's worth fighting for, it's worth fighting for*. Grandpa said that she was worth every bit of effort and time (seventy years). What a perfect fit they are!

The boy turned home, eager to tell of his time with the old man as he relayed the stories that he could remember, especially why there are thirteen steps going upstairs. He could fool the other kids with that one. And he needed an ego boost. Everyone called him *Little Willie*. But what he didn't know was that he would be 6'4" tall by the time he was fourteen.

But at this point, he envied his cousin that lived up the street. He had always been *The Boy*, robust and athletic. The two boys lived across the street from one another and were very close. Often Grandpa would ask, *What're Little Willie and the Boy doing? I hope they're looking out for one another, especially that skinny one.* Then Grandpa would follow with – *when I was that age* – and tell of the time that he saved his little brother from drowning.

"I was skinnier than you back then," Grandpa said. "But when my brother went under the raft at Waterloo swimming hole and couldn't get out, I jumped right in and pulled him out. So don't you worry about being bony. Just be strong and ready to do what is necessary." Willie felt better after that.

Willie decided right there and then that he would visit Grandpa every day if possible. He wanted to know more about the old days and what Grandpa did and what he was like back then. Like the time he was the only child in the 5th grade at school, the first time he talked on the telephone, his first kiss, how to cure athlete's foot, how to shoot a shotgun, why moss grows on only one side of a tree (and which side is that?). Good to know if you get lost in the woods.

Willie also wanted to know how to knock almonds, run an almond huller, pick strawberries and potatoes, herd sheep, shine shoes, brush a daughter's hair, be a boss, tie a tie, drive a stick shift car, change a diaper, count money; and much, much, more. Grandpa knows all that kind of stuff.

While the boy was trying to digest all that, he was jolted from his thoughts when the voice of the old man rang in his ears: *Most of all, my boy—love and be loved. Love intensely.*

This reminded the boy of something that Grandpa said once before: *There are three kinds of love.* Like when Mommy and Daddy fall in love and start a family. And like when you have a baby brother or any family member or a friend. And then there is love like you have for chocolate cake and little puppies. Love all these ways, my boy. It will take you a long, long way.

The little boy is grown up now. He often thinks of Grandpa, wishing he were young again, sitting at Grandpa's feet, listening to more stories.

But he doesn't have to wish. A young boy sits at his feet, amazed at the things that (as he was told) came from generations past, and now handed down to another.

But what about the story? The old man, in the wisdom of his years, leaves the conclusion to the hearer. *Better imagined than said,* was the old man's final words.

Perhaps there will be another tomorrow, in another place, another time, another Grandpa, another story.

Let's hope so!

And a Farewell Poem

Here I sit broken-hearted;

knowing soon we will be parted.

It took me years to write this book,

Please give it more than just a look

Ask yourself, was this about me?

Or someone I know?

Read it again!

Let the words simply flow.

Was it excitement?

Or an indictment?

I had fun in writing.

I hope you did in reading.

So, I say goodbye to you,

and I say it pleading.

Many thanks to my family and friends who encouraged
me to write this book,
and to Susan for editorial expertise.

About the Author

The middle of five active boys, Douglas A. Alberts was born in Northern Minnesota. When he was two, his folks left the cold (for which, he always said, he was very grateful, as the cold chills him to the bone) heading West for new opportunities and settled on the Pacific Coast. After graduation from a Central California Valley high school, Doug joined the U.S. Air Force and was inspired to jot poetry and prose on tiny scraps of paper. Following military service, he married, fathered three children, and began his rewarding career in ministry. Retirement provided time for reflection on life's joys and losses, organization of those paper bits, and thoughtful expressions of life filled with wisdom and humor. New experiences, a new marriage, and regular trips between coasts give Doug new prospects for exciting new writings.